The Bandit of Bloody Run

Center Point
Large Print

Also by Nelson Nye and available from
Center Point Large Print:

The Shootin' Sheriff

**This Large Print Book carries the
Seal of Approval of N.A.V.H.**

The Bandit of Bloody Run

Nelson Nye

CENTER POINT LARGE PRINT
THORNDIKE, MAINE

This Center Point Large Print edition is published
in the year 2013 by arrangement with
Golden West Literary Agency.

The text of this Large Print edition is unabridged.
In other aspects, this book may
vary from the original edition.
Printed in the United States of America
on permanent paper.
Set in 16-point Times New Roman type.

ISBN: 978-1-61173-686-1

Library of Congress Cataloging-in-Publication Data

Nye, Nelson C. (Nelson Coral), 1907-1997.
The bandit of Bloody Run / Nelson Nye.
pages ; cm.
ISBN 978-1-61173-686-1 (library binding : alk. paper)
1. Large type books. I. Title.
PS3527.Y33B34 2013
813'.54—dc23

2012042242

I

The Sound of Hurried Hoofs

"String 'im up an' get it over with!"

If the ominous words reached Tucker Hart, he gave no sign. Beneath the lone cottonwood dominating this small clearing, he sat his horse in stoical silence. It was late fall and a biting frost was in the air. Yet old Hart sat there calmly, once or twice raising a cold blue hand to rasp his chin.

An ironic gleam perceptibly deepened in his eyes as the ring of men closed round him.

"It's high time these long-ridin' sons was made t' savvy rustlin' ain't declarin' dividends," growled Sumptor, owner of the Lazy D. "They're bad in need of a good example—an' I propose t' see they git one!"

A plump smile spread across his shaved-hog face. He said in a tone of satisfaction: "Hart, yo're goin' to hang."

Sardonic humor streaked the prisoner's gaze. Looked like this yammering pack of coyotes figured they were being plenty smart.

Sumptor said with mock solicitude: "Y'u want we should give yore kid any message?"

Hart grinned sourly. "Might tell him," he said, "I expect the climate's better back in Wyomin'."

There was something fine in the tilt of Hart's old head, in the straightness of his back as he sat surrounded by his enemies. Regardless of all that was held against him, despite those ruthless measures he had sometimes used to gain his power, here sat the last of the great cattle barons. No throne under heaven was ever made or held without the shedding of blood. Whatever men might say of Tucker Hart, none had ever cause to name him coward or weakling.

He wheeled his shaggy head around to scan these faces. It almost seemed that he was etching them in mind against some future need. Snake Dunkett with his hatchet face a mask of triumph. Kinch Lee, tall, gangling, mocking. Deuces Darst, his gambler's eyes inscrutable as the pallid cheeks below them. And Sumptor with his plump face of a shaven hog.

Roosting vultures waiting for the kill.

Hart spoke softly and with dry earnestness. "I 'low you fellas know I'm innocent—so we'll let that pass. I'm no man to waste my breath. You've gathered round to gloat an' watch a fella mortal take the jump. So cackle hearty, buzzards. Before the month's out, ev'ry mother's son of you'll come taggin' me down the Boothill trail."

With snarled curses Lee and Dunkett threw their weight against the rope. Sumptor's quirt tore a whistling V. With a forward hurtling lunge, Hart's horse shot out from under.

The lash of hoof sound rolled from the flanking timber.

Someone whirled with a startled curse. The healthy color drained from Dunkett's face as with a squeal of fear he scuttled for his horse. Nor did his companions show a greater wish to linger.

They were gone in a rush of thunder, leaving the little park deserted save for that motionless figure that eerily creaked at a rope's end as the chill wind swayed it to and fro.

II

All Roads Lead to Gunplay

"Son, you got the blood of heroes in yore veins," one of the County Commissioners told Ten-Horse Jones. "I mean it, boy! We're expectin' great things from you. Yore ol' man was knowed as a holy terror when he was roddin' Tombstone. An', while we ain't honin' t' see you turnin' Hudspeth County into no damn shambles, we sure are countin' on seein' the place cleaned up. There's too dang many sidewinders makin' this place their sunnin' ground; we want the custom stopped. We're givin' you a free hand an' we'll back you all the way—all we're askin' is results."

Ten-Horse Jones—so-called because of his phobia for keeping that many sleek and fast-stepping range broncs always under saddle— grinned. "Shucks," he said, "I reckon you are overratin' my ability consid'rable. But you can count on me t' do my best."

"I'm sure of it," declared the County Commissioner. "You'll stick with this chore till hell freezes—an' then skate with it across the ice. You're a stubborn whelp. The kind I like." He cleared his throat. "Now hoist yore paw an' I'll swear you in."

Jones did so, and the C.C. pinned the sheriff's badge upon his calfskin vest.

That had been two weeks ago. Since then he had twice loaded the up-bound stage with tinhorns and minor outlaws, and had speeded them toward other pastures with an earnest admonition to see to it that their shadows did not darken Hudspeth County ground again. He had fired some shots which—although their echoes might not have gone clean round the world—had certainly got a pair of tough gunslammers a more or less permanent rest in Eagle Flat's boothill. He had discouraged sundry unwonted drifters from dropping their picket pins in his locality. Besides these things, not at all inconsiderable in themselves, he had fitted a softer pedal to Jeff Morris' Striped Tiger Bar, and had openly hinted that if Morris' customers didn't conduct themselves with more decorum in the very immediate future he'd thin them out.

All in all, it was a good beginning.

Ten-Horse prepared to do a little resting on his laurels.

Up the Eagle Flat trail from Allamoore and Wild Horse rode a solitary horseman. A short and chunky fellow with a straw-colored mustache decorating the dried-apple features beneath his dusty San An hat.

"Cripes," the horseman muttered after running his hands through several pockets. "No smoke, no job, an' dang little dinero. It looks, hawse, like the poorhouse was plumb starin' us in the eye! An' a dang fine fix in which fer a man like me tuh find hisself!"

After a time he added lugubriously: "Special' a fella what's used tuh bein' the pride of forty-eight states—not tuh mention *You*-rope!"

Half an hour later he entered the horse-tracked dust of Eagle Flat's main street and tossed his reins across a tie-rack. Swinging down, he clumped his frazzled boots toward a building bearing the weathered sign: ALAMO RESTAURANT.

He stepped inside and for several exhilarating moments stood gawping at the girl behind the counter. She was, he thought, a ravishing beauty —"prettier'n a spotted dawg under a red wagon!" Her creamy skin held the luster of polished ivory, and her hair was sleek and black as any raven's wing; black as the long lashes framing her sparkly eyes. And her lips!—the stranger's heart accelerated tempo at the very thought!

He finally summoned presence of mind enough to take a stool at the counter and mumble his order, craning his neck to follow her with his eyes until the closing kitchen door cut off his view. When she put the meal before him he ate it, and never afterward was able to recall what it consisted of. Its taste, he swore, was like a nectar of the gods!

He finished, wiped his mouth on a paper napkin, and paid his bill with the last of his remaining shekels. Then he favored the pretty waitress with what he believed to be an engaging smile. "Any jobs driftin' round here footloose?"

"If you're a man of action—sure. Got a job right up your alley, Stranger. The Sheriff's short a deputy and'll probably be glad to put you on."

"Deputy! Hell's hinges, gal, I been a deppity fer ten long wasted years! Ain't they nothin' else round here fer a man tuh try? Change is what I need!"

She regarded him with something like a pitying smile. "You couldn't land a job on a cow outfit lookin' like you do," she told him. "These ranchers are wanting gun fighters. You look more like a grub-line rider. You better brace the Sheriff."

The stranger sighed. "Looks like talent is plumb wasted in this country—"

"What kinda talent you packin', Stranger?"

The little man whirled like a spur-bit bronc. One hand flapped to the Colt that sagged his sawed-off holster. But, just in time, he seemed to catch the glint of metal on the newcomer's vest, and dropped the hand aside with a sheepish grin.

"Shucks," he muttered. "I sure thought fer a minute yuh might be one of them fresh young cowprods what's allus lookin' tuh haze ever' stranger that comes ridin' in. You the gent what's lookin' fer the deppity?"

The newcomer nodded, grinning.

The girl displayed her smile impartially. "Ten-Horse," she said, "meet—uh, er—"

"Kasta—Pony George Kasta," announced the shabbily-dressed stranger with an air. He doffed his hat to the waitress, adding, "Yuh'll be hearin' more o' me before long, ma'am."

Again her white teeth sparkled between the redness of her parted lips. Mr. Kasta appeared to find her downright attractive. He looked at her admiringly and his Adam's apple—never a restive organ at best—performed gymnastics. He roused from his trance to hear her saying "this is Ten-Horse Jones, the sheriff of Hudspeth County."

"Glad t' know you," Ten-Horse said, grabbing his hand and pumping it.

"Same tuh you," gasped Pony George, wriggling his fingers experimentally and relieved to find them still in working order after the lawman's vigorous clasp.

"Had any experience in the sheriffin' business?"

"Experience! My sainted aunt! Young fella, I been packin' a star fer goin' on eleven years—'leven years come grass."

"Fine," observed Ten-Horse, grinning. "Just the hombre I need. About this—ah, 'talent' you was mentionin' . . . ?"

"I'm knowed," George said, "as the 'Lawman Poet of Pecos,'" and stuck out his chest importantly.

"Poet, eh?" The sheriff's tone seemed cooler. "Won't have a deal of time to exercise that talent round here, I'm 'fraid. Ever know a fella over at Pecos called Lawler?"

"Red Lawler!" George chuckled. "I sh'ld say so! Worked with him an' Anders."

"How come you quit?"

"Didn't!" George denied. "I give them dang Commissioners the ten best years of my life! I risked more dang peril defendin' the tax-payers' money than yuh could shake a stick at! What did I get fer it? Nothin', by cripes! They made me actin'-sheriff when Anders quit, an' when it come time fer me t' git my hard-earned raise they up an' booted me outen the office! Helluva way t' treat a man what's never took a bribe an' has allus done his duty as he seen it, irregardless of whose pet corns got tromped on!"

Ten-Horse shoved back his hat and roughed his yellow hair. He was a tall, gaunt man with a hard but likable grin. But he was not grinning now. He

12

cuffed the hat back down again and rasped a hand across his jaw, regarding the ex-sheriff of Pecos somewhat dubiously. "Well," he said at last, "I expect I can use you. There's a lot t' do around this town an' I can't be here all the time. It's a twenty-four hour job, the way things been shapin' up. Come over to the office an' I'll swear you in."

"Here—hold on!" growled Mr. Kasta. "I ain't plumb sure I want that job. What happened to the last incumbent?"

"Krail? He had to shoot a fella," the sheriff said reluctantly, "an' after the funeral the fella's friends got together an' rubbed 'im out."

George scowled. "Daggone," he said with exasperation; "now I think of it, I'm 'fraid that job ain't fer me after all." He swallowed uncomfortably as he caught the waitress' eyes upon him. "Jest recollected I promised tuh meet a fella over to El Paso—"

"You're not *afraid* to work for Ten-Horse, are you?" the girl broke in.

"Afraid! Who—*me?*" Pony George glowered indignantly. "I sh'd say not! I'm knowed as the fightin'est star-packer in fifty-seven counties—not mentionin' Canada! I been called the 'Hound of the Law,' I'll hev you know! An'—"

"Ten-Horse," she said plaintively, "sure needs a man like you. He ain't been gettin' much cooperation lately, and the commissioners—"

"Say no more!" George stopped her solemnly.

13

"Commissioners, is it? Why, to spite them buzzards I'd sling coal fer the devil! Lead on, Jones, an' get that swearin' over!"

They sat a spell in silence. Ten-Horse chucked some fodder in the stove and George spread his gnarled hands above its top appreciatively. "It's sure gettin' colder'n a frog's belly. Mebbe you ort t' put me wise to what's goin' on around this neck of the woods if I'm goin' to be of any help to yuh."

"Oh, there ain't much doin' at the moment," Ten-Horse said. "Been a couple cow outfits feudin' round a spell over water rights an' fences—but it don't amount to much. Been a mite of rustlin', too—but that ain't a heap unusual. Mostly folks is gettin' riled about this fella they call the Bandit of Bloody Run, account of he holes up someplace in a canyon by that name over round Tabernacle Mountain.

"Some two-bit bad man tryin' to get a cheap rep by stickin' up the El Paso stage. Made two-three pretty fair hauls. Killed a man last week. I'll say this for him—he's plenty slick. That's why I been keen on gettin' me a new deputy. Got t' hunt that fella down an' I ain't cravin' t' leave this section without no law while them ranchers is paintin' up for war."

"Bandit of Bloody Run?" A far-away look got into the eyes of Pony George.

Jones said, "Humph! What that fella needs—" and stopped, turning a narrowed stare upon the door.

A rataplan of hoofbeats stopped outside. A rider's boots hit dirt. The same boots beat three staccato sounds from the board walk. Then the door was flung violently open.

Lamplight showed the dusty features of a wild-eyed man who raked the office with a piercing gaze. "He's done it now!" he shouted at the sheriff. "Damn' skunk stopped 'er this side of Lasca, cracked the box, an' got away with the thirty thousan' bein' shipped the Del Rio bank!"

III

"I Got a Murder on My Hands!"

Slow Jim Hart laid down his fork and listened. His ears had caught the muffled pounding of a fast-running horse. He leaned forward, canting his head as the sounds drew rapidly nearer.

"Now what's up?" he scowled. "Always somethin' goin' wrong around this haywire outfit!"

In a crunching skid the hoofbeats ceased before the porch. Booted feet rushed up the steps and the door slammed open. Young Jim stared.

A panting man stood framed in the ranch house doorway. His hat was gone. His hair was tousled and excitement burned in his widened eyes.

"Shorty! What ails you?"

The chunky rider got his breath. "Jim!—*Jim!*" he gasped. "They've hung yore ol' man!"

For slow-ticked seconds a crouching silence gripped the room.

Slow Jim's chair crashed to the floor as he got abruptly to his feet, his meal forgotten. He towered above the puncher, shaking him savagely.

"Who is *they?*"

"That gol-rammed Lazy D bunch! Who else would hev the nerve t' pull as raw a stunt as that? Tumbleweed Sumptor an' his crowd, an' Deuces Darst from Eagle Flat. Found one of them brass tags like the Ol' Man's chaps is decorated with. Claimed they picked it up on the bedground of that Bar X herd what was rustled the other night. Kinch Lee swore the Ol' Man's been bossin' them rustlers all along!"

So his father had been hanged! This was the culmination of the bad feeling aroused by that unpleasantness over water rights and fences.

Muscles tightened along Slow Jim's lean jaw.

A lone wolf, old Tucker Hart. But it was known that Jim had worshiped him on a par with God.

Jim's opaque, smoke-colored eyes stared fixedly at the expectant puncher. Shorty Hebron was shiftless by nature and dirty by habit—a man could almost see Slow Jim's mind working; it

16

were as though he were asking himself 'Could such a man be trusted?'

Under the young ranchman's steady regard Hebron shuffled his feet uneasily. "They hung 'im, Jim," he repeated insistently. "They sure did—I saw 'em at it. Then I beat it straight fer here."

The oppressive hush closed down again. Slow Jim appeared to be doing some thinking. Probably brooding, Hebron thought, over the way they'd framed his Dad. He recalled how Slow Jim had more than once warned the Ol' Man against Kinch Lee—yeah, and against that paunchy Sumptor, too!

Slow Jim said: "Shorty, are yuh shore Darst was in this?"

"Deuces? Didn't I see 'im with my own eyes? Hell, yes, he was there!"

"Hmm . . . That would seem t' be conclusive," Slow Jim murmured, and appeared to be weighing the puncher's statement.

After a moment he pried the cork from a bottle, proffering it with a glass. "Darst's a tinhorn; he ain't no cowman. What would he be mixin' in this for?"

"A tinhorn, yeah—an' the boss of Eagle Flat." A cunning gleam lighted Shorty's eyes as he poured himself three fingers of the bottle's contents. He downed it at a gulp. "I'll tell yuh somethin'," he said, leaning forward impressively.

"Darst, Kinch Lee, an' Sumptor's a dang sight thicker'n most folks figger—thicker'n splatter, if yuh're askin' *me!* Allus meetin' up someplace where there ain't nobody apt tuh see 'em. Layin' pipe fer somethin'. Keep yore eyes skinned out fer them hombres!"

Slow Jim nodded noncommittally. But some faint gleam in his eye said he found this knowledge of more than ordinary worth. A man might almost have said it convinced him of something he had already definitely suspected.

He stretched up a hand and lifted down a gunbelt from its peg against the wall. "Now where's that knife?" he muttered, and—"Oh! I'd plumb fergot about that. . . ." He noticed the watching puncher and closed his mouth. Grunting, he strapped the belt with its holstered .45 about his narrow waist.

Hebron grinned. This was something like it. 'Course, the young fool wouldn't stand no more chance against Sumptor's crowd than a jackrabbit would against buckshot. But that was Slow Jim's lookout. It promised to be interesting.

Hebron said, "I knowed yuh wouldn't let them guys git away with it," and smirked suggestively. He had long ago decided Hart was a plain brash fool.

But Slow Jim's expelled breath cut short his grin. "I'm goin' out an' cut Dad down," he said, with a short harsh laugh at Hebron's expression.

"Don't go jumpin' at conclusions. I ain't figurin' t' go hoppin' Sumptor's bunch—you can ditch that notion right now. I don't see it that way nohow."

Jaw slack, Hebron stared. "What'll Tony say?"

Slow Jim's smoky eyes grew narrow. Some inner thinking spread a film of caution across his gaze. "Reckon she'd be wantin' me t' come gunnin' her Dad?" he said.

But Hebron countered with a positive statement. "Yuh can't back down, Jim. It's the code!"

"Then damn the code! I'm pullin' out."

Hebron's jaw dropped lower. His eyes bulged incredulously.

Slow Jim's laugh was a brittle, mirthless sound. "Wake up, you fool! I ain't honin' t' be no hero. Hell! One death in this family's a-plenty!"

The puncher stared with hot, accusing eyes. "Cripes!" he said, and "Cripes! I thought you was a Texan!"

Slow Jim shoved the bottle at him. "Pour yourself a stiff one—it sure looks like you need it."

Hebron did so, his bug-eyed glance staying bewilderedly on Hart. He dragged the back of a hand across his mouth. "Cripes," he muttered; "I don't get it. A Tehanner—an' no damn sand in his craw!"

"C'mon, let's go!" cried Pony George, hitching at his gunbelt. "If it's that pilgrim over at Bloody

Run this fella's speelin' about, I say let's git him dead tuh rights!"

Ten-Horse waggled an irritable hand. "Keep your trousers on," he said and tapped the dottle from his pipe, reloading it with exasperating slowness. "Don't never do no leapin' round this office till you see what you got ahead of you. This deal's got a number of possibilities."

He looked at the man who'd brought the tidings. "I'm swearin' you in, Shortridge. Hold up your hand."

And after the swearing was over, Ten-Horse said: "Go down to the pool room and Jeff Morris' Striped Tiger Bar an' see can you round me up a posse. I'll meet you at the livery in ten minutes."

Shortridge departed on the run.

Pony George screwed up his dried-apple countenance into a reflective scowl. "Seems like this place's gettin' 'bout as bad as Pecos fer excitement. They been raisin' tough eggs s' fast over there, they ain't no room fer honest gents tuh set their feet."

"You got somethin' there," Ten-Horse muttered. Getting down to business, he added: "I got to get after that Bloody Run vinegarone. I'm goin' to leave you in charge here an' I want you t' keep the lid on tight. Any of these tough brush-poppers give you any mouth, just slap 'em in the brisket an' stick 'em in the cooler till they sing a diff'rent tune. Don't mess with 'em. Look for me when you see me." He started for the door.

"Hold on," George grunted. Pretty certain that Ten-Horse had definitely made up his mind and was not to be argued from his purpose, he said reproachfully: "I was kinda hopin' to go 'long with yuh. Seems kinda foolish fer yuh to be leavin' a fightin' man like me behind. Cripes, been so long since I've had a decent chance t' unlimber my artillery, 'twouldn't su'prise me none t' find my bangin' finger goin' stiff. I—"

"You stand pat," Jones bade him, grinning wryly. "This town's good for all you want t' see —an' somethin' over, mebbe." And, still grinning, he passed out into the desert night.

"Now what'd he mean by that crack?" George demanded, frowning. "An' why the hell can't some guys ever learn t' close a door?"

He kicked the offending barrier shut and resumed his seat beside the stove. Gusty wind was pulling whining sound from the building's eaves. He was quite content, despite his lament to Ten-Horse, to stay in this snug office.

Seemed like Fate had once again projected him into a situation holding scant attraction to a man of peace and rectitude. No shrinking violet, George was none the less partial to the pleasanter sides of life. He'd viewed all the gore he wanted under Lawler and Colt Anders. He felt he'd earned a rest—only trouble was he couldn't find a sponsor willing to put up the price for resting.

He got up at last and went rummaging through the sheriff's desk. In a drawer sandwiched between a bunch of pigeon holes he found what he was after. A nice light tan cigar. He did not hesitate, but peeled its cellophane wrapper off at once and inside of five seconds was puffing like a plutocrat.

He went back to his seat beside the stove.

He took a long, appreciative drag from the inspiring cigar he'd purloined from the sheriff's desk. "Expect I'm about—"

The cigar went off with a loud report!

Rearing up in startled alarm, Pony George pawed wildly at his face and mustache. This was not a real sane thing to do, considering that his chair was balanced on two legs only, whilst his own legs were propped against an open drawer of the sheriff's desk.

The drawer slammed shut and the chair went over backward. In a splintering crash it struck the iron footrail encircling the stove's bottom. With a tinny wrenching sound, the stovepipe let go its hold upon the ceiling and came toppling, its fall obscured by billowing clouds of soot but its landing—while not happy—plainly audible.

Pony George, feeling strangely like a fool, and mad enough to chew railroad spikes, shoved a portion of stovepipe off one shoulder, disentangled his neck and Adam's apple from a mangled section of chair, and struggled to his feet leaking soot from every joint and wrinkle.

Blowing like a porpoise, he pulled a chair leg from his boot and three slats from the waistband of his trousers and heaved them through the window. The tinkling of the shattered glass reminded him that it had not been open.

He seemed to realize suddenly that the cause of all this trouble was the choice cigar still gripped between his teeth. He pulled it from his mouth, eying its ragged end vindictively. With a righteous oath he hurled it after the evicted bits of chair, and stamped across the office.

"Sure looks like Ol' Home Week in Hell," he muttered disgustedly.

He was mightily tempted to unpin his star and head forthwith for other parts. All that stopped him was the timely reflection that without money he could not get very far—

He got down on one knee presently and attempted to fit the broken chair together. Seemed like, though, the thing had had four legs originally. The back, too, had shown a different contour.

A lucky thought clicked over in his mind and he dragged a sleeve across his sweaty face. That Ten-Horse fella wasn't going to like the look of things—there was no gainsaying that!

"I expect," he said, "I better do a *good* job while I'm at it."

He picked up the chair and hurled it at the sheriff's desk. The result was all he could have hoped for. "Reckon that'll look convincin'."

With a saturnine grin he hitched up his belt and went outside. Just because this place looked like the morning-after-the-night-before, he reflected philosophically, was no good why he shouldn't polish off the rest of that dang trick cigar.

He was on his eighth match and bending over like a hound on a hot scent, when he became aware that he was not alone. There was another croucher on this campus; he stood with arms akimbo watching George as though he guessed he'd taken leave of his senses. "What y'u lost, pal?" this fellow said.

"A damn good snipe!" George answered grumpily, and picked up the errant cigar. "D'yuh think I was huntin' nightcrawlers?"

Straightening, he lifted the Bowie knife from his boot and sliced off the tattered section which had held the jokester's cap. Then he lit up. After he got it going good he felt a little better.

"What was you lookin' fer?" he asked.

"I was wonderin' if the sheriff was around."

"He ain't—but you're lookin' at the greatest lawgiver since the days of Moses," George said modestly. "I'm the chief deppity. What can I do yuh fer?"

"Wal," the other man said a little dubiously. "I got a murder on my hands. I wonder if you'd mind comin' down an' lookin' round?"

IV

The Hound of the Law

Shortly after Ten-Horse Jones had galloped out of town at the head of his hastily-collected posse, other folk began an in-drift, congregating sooner or later before Jeff Morris' Striped Tiger Bar. In a half hour quite a crowd had gathered and was being steadily augmented by new arrivals.

There was more than ordinary reason for this gathering. To be sure, a dance—or *stomp,* in cowboy parlance—was to be held inside its spacious walls this night. And a dance to the folk who live on isolated ranches was a social event of supreme importance. But its importance on this occasion was considerably enhanced by the fact that its sponsor was no less a person than Deuces Darst, self-styled boss of Eagle Flat.

He had not bothered to send out invitations—but none was really necessary. In Texas, to hear that a stomp was being held was to consider oneself invited.

So they came from miles around. In buggies, spring wagons, buckboards, on horseback and in tin lizzies. They came not out of courtesy to Deuces Darst—leastways not the cowboys; but rather because no one cared to miss an affair of this magnitude. The ladies arrived in taffetas, silks, and satins; the gents came in go-t'hell britches and fancy silk shirts. No one appeared to give a hoot for the fact that long rides over dusty trails might dull their pristine splendor. No one, that is, save Antonia Sumptor. She brought her party clothes along in a go-Easter and looked for a secluded spot to get into the things after her arrival. She came with her father's range boss, Bill McCash, who was a hard-case hombre with a profile and ready fists and plenty able to get her all the privacy she wanted.

Neighbors met for the first time in many weeks. Old animosities—if not forgotten—were temporarily held in leash. Folks came for an evening's fun and frolic.

Along the inside of the Striped Tiger's walls, planks and boxes had been placed for the womenfolks. Not that they were destined to enjoy these long! Folks were yet to see the time when any woman could be a wallflower at a stomp in Eagle Flat—most of them felt lucky when they could dodge a set and rest.

The fiddler thumped his strings and the affair got off to a lively start.

Though he had not said anything about it, Ten-Horse had been plenty peeved at missing this occasion, and spending the night instead on a wild hunt for that two-bit stage robber. Dances were few and far between and Ten-Horse had been looking forward to this one as a chance to get within shouting distance of Sumptor's ravishing daughter. He'd have long since gotten closer to her than that, only for the fact of Slow Jim Hart's having an inside track with her, and Slow Jim once having been his pardner.

Already Slow Jim and Bill McCash had tangled over the right to win her regard. And were like to tangle again, McCash was hinting, if Hart didn't mind his own damned business!

Perhaps that accounted for Slow Jim's absence from this stomp. There were people here who thought so.

But 'Tonia did not lack for ready admirers. The stag line glowered as she took the floor with McCash.

The boss fiddler, Lazy Bill, kept time with every appendage on his body—head, hands, feet; and grinned like a soused hyena. His boys all played by 'ear' and their varied variations were a thing to listen to. But they could play by the hour (and longer, if they had a drink!) and nobody knew the difference if they did scramble the melody a mite.

The 'caller' was a leather-lunged jasper with a mouth that could have swallowed Jonah's whale. He was a forward gent and plenty familiar, as he'd been told more than once. Mostly he called from memory, but when that got a little rusty he was not averse to ringing in some variations of his own.

At eleven by the fly-specked clock above the bar, a shot rang out, its sharp report plainly heard above the noise.

Fiddles sawed to a wailing stop. A mouthharp left its melody up among the rafters. Old Lazy Bill stopped off balance and stayed that way with mouth agape. Dancers were thrown into confusion as the line of men standing along the south wall broke for the door.

Every gent in that hall seemed positive his last chance for heaven depended on his getting to the outside first.

But Deuces Darst managed to beat them all.

He thrust aggressively through the hastily-gathering crowd, shoving men off his elbows without regard of what they thought about it. "Back up!" he growled authoritatively.

"Some fella downed Snake Dunkett!"

Darst reached the inner circle with Jeff Morris treading on his heels. Both men came to an abrupt stop. Morris took one look and strode away with his lips tight shut. Dunkett lay on the ground in a strangely twisted manner.

Swiftly Darst dropped to a knee beside him. He had seen what others evidently hadn't. Dunkett was not yet dead.

Gazing down into those up-turned terror-filled eyes, Darst felt a chill of premonition. Dunkett's lips were moving. Darst leaned close.

"Demon from hell! Demon from hell!" rasped

the tired lips feebly. "Gawd, Deuces—I seen Black Death a-horseback! . . . Black—"

"Damn fool!" Darst muttered as the faint voice ceased. "Never did have the brain capacity of a flea!"

He turned, raising a peremptory hand for silence. "Who saw this shootin'?"

No one spoke and Darst said, "Well?" sharply. "Somebody must of got a look at that killer! Talk up!"

"Black-garbed gent on a big roan geldin'. Couldn't git a look at his pan. Kept too much in the shadder an' had his hat pulled down."

Darst eyed the speaker intently. "What started it?"

"I don't rightly know. Dunkett was sayin' as how some fellas strung up ol' Tucker Hart las' night. Claimed he was a rustler an' was responsible fer all the stock that's been sproutin' wings lately. 'Twas Dunkett's notion every cow-thief in the country oughta be given a swig from the same bottle. 'Bout that time, here comes that black-garbed gent, ridin' up kinder slow an' easy-like. Jest set there eyin' Snake an' not lettin' out a peep. Dunkett seen him after a minute an' says real proddy: 'Well, damn yuh, don't yuh like it?' "

"Yeah? Keep talkin'," Darst grumbled impatiently.

"Would," the man retorted, " 'f you'd give me haff a chanct. The black horseman jest sat his saddle, not movin' an' not sayin' nothin', but jest starin' cold at Dunkett. Gawd, it fair give me the creeps the way he set there. But when he spoke it was a dang sight worse! Voice made a fella kinda reconsider hell—it was that harsh an' raspy-like. 'Dunkett, yuh rat, yo're first,' he says, real slow an' spooky.

"But Dunkett, he begun backin' off, snarlin' an' glarin'. His gun han' kep' openin' an' closin' like he was cravin' tuh grab iron. But you could see he didn't dare.

"An' then suddenly he did. Out come his gun a-spoutin'. He shore got in first shot. But that was all, an' it didn't do him no manner o' good. That fella jest set his saddle, starin'—with his head tipped kinda for'ard. You could see them eyes a-glowin' like hot coals beneath his hatbrim. Then his arm shot out an' Dunkett fell with a knife in his chest—same one you see there now. The fella rode off laffin'."

"Laffin', eh?"

Darst hooked his thumbs in the armholes of his fancy vest. Silent, he stood quite still, his gaze going first to the speaker and then to Dunkett's body. "Snake," he asked finally, "got any relatives you gents ever heard of?"

Nobody answered.

Darst's shoulders stirred impatiently. "Well, take him down to the Sheriff's Office—don't leave him layin' here." Stooping, he pulled the heavy blade from Dunkett's chest.

"Somebody hunt up the coroner. This thing'll have to be looked into."

His eyes went across the silent gathering, then he turned and strode away.

The crowd broke up.

The dance did, too.

"Here—what's this?" demanded Pony George, clutching his companion's arm.

"It looks," said Morris, peering, "mighty like the victim. . . . Yeah, I reckon it is. Name's Dunkett—'Snake' fer short."

"Wal, suff'rin' sidewinders! You can't bring no corpse up here! I won't hev it! I—"

He gulped, leaving the rest unsaid as the four men toting Dunkett's body pulled up before him, staring.

"Now look," he muttered wrathily; "where d'ye reckon yuh're a-fetchin' that dang stiff?"

"Sheriff's Office," vouchsafed the foremost man laconically.

"Not by a jugful! I'll be danged ef yuh are! Yuh turn right round an' take him back where yuh got him!"

"I guess not," George's companion said.

George was getting mad. "An' who are you?"

But the fellow had dealt with madder men than him—and showed it. "I'm Jeff Morris," he answered softly. "An' can pull my weight in any crowd. These boys picked Dunkett up in front of my saloon. There's no sense arguin', Mister. I got a hard enough time makin' a livin' now without havin' no damn stiff impedin' trade."

"Then take him to the coroner's—you can't plant him in *my* office!"

The dead man's carriers looked inquiringly at Morris.

Morris shrugged. "You can take him to El Paso fer all of me."

"Hold on!" growled George as the saloonman started off. "I got some questions yuh can answer—"

"You the sheriff?" Morris asked insultingly.

"No. But I'm chief deppity, an'—"

"Then I'll point out I been asked a heap of questions in my time an' never answered any yet." Morris looked at him and sneered.

"Yuh'll answer mine!" growled George, and jabbed a pistol into Morris' paunch.

Morris let out a grunt of pain. It was mingled with amazement.

George was some amazed himself. He hadn't known such courage was in him—but saw no reason for telling the saloonman that. "Jest lay a track fer my office, Mister," he drawled; "—an' lay it quick!"

The corpse brigade got under way, moving—if the truth be told—considerably faster than they had been doing before George stopped them.

Morris, with a muttered oath, turned toward the sheriff's office.

V

"He Ain't Got No Guts!"

Ten-Horse Jones was one of those good-natured, easy-going people who had never been known to take things seriously—least of all himself. Aside from his ten fast horses, all he could lay claim to was on his back, and it was quite apparent that he was satisfied with his lot. Very probably he had never felt the itch to better it; or, if he had, was too fool lazy to go to that much trouble.

But if he was content with life as he found it, there were those in Hudspeth County who very definitely were not. They intended taking him in hand, both for his good and their own.

As the County Commissioner had intimated, he had been put into office because important people were convinced that he was just the man to carry out their wishes—and their strongest wish was to see the law enforced.

Upon a number of recalled occasions these people had seen Jones 'get his mad up.' They had been impressed, for the occasions had been a caution to certain gentlemen no longer dwelling in those parts. Solid citizens had not forgotten, and it was their contention that, given a star, proper coaching, and a fine tradition to uphold,

Ten-Horse Jones could be a lawman to make history. They had gone to the polls to prove it and had given him the election by an overwhelming vote.

Tall, gaunt, and yellow haired, his appearance was compatible with his easy-going nature—which was too well known to admit of doubt. All the crooks in Hudspeth County had helped to get him victory with their ballots; and had none-too-secretly congratulated one another on the opportunity.

But solid citizens recalled times when Ten-Horse's long wide lips had lost their customary whimsicality, had gone grim and hard above his stubborn jaw and streaked a smile that in itself had been all the warning needed by certain hombres 'no longer with us.' Respectable sponsors of Mr. Jones appeared well-content with their selection. With gleaming eyes they slapped each other on the back and chuckled.

And not without good reason.

Ten-Horse Jones had one dangerous weakness —a cold and deadly temper that took no account of either obstacles or odds in righting anything conceived by him to be a personal affront. He knew a bit of Scripture and was a staunch adherent to that bit.

To Hudspeth County undesirables, the new sheriff was just a lazy, brush-popping cowpoke; an ideal man to pack the badge of high authority.

Slow to rile, easy-going, caring little for what went on so long as his toes were not stepped on, he was a familiar figure round the poker tables of the Striped Tiger Bar; a man who could be 'touched' by anyone, and easily induced to spend his wages buying liquor for the crowd.

But—and this *they did not know*—with the Old Testament, Jones believed in an 'eye for an eye.' Jones, in fact, went further—he believed in a leg for an ankle, a hideful of broken ribs for a bloody nose, and boothill for the man who laid hands on another gent's horse!

It was 4 p.m. when Ten-Horse came jogging back to town next day at the head of his weary posse. That the Bandit of Bloody Run had gotten clear was amply evidenced by the expressions of their faces.

Dismissing his disgruntled helpers, and mentally resolved to have no more to do with them, he racked his horse before the restaurant and went inside to feed his face.

He was tired—but not too tired to note the gleam of excitement in the biscuit-shooter's eyes.

"What'll you have, Ten-Horse?"

He read a shade of difference in the smile she gave him. It was not the one she customarily turned on.

He said, "I'll take the news first, Tessie—"

"News, sir? What news is that?"

35

"Skip it, sister, an' get down to bedrock," Ten-Horse growled. "What's up?"

"Well—" she loosed an excited giggle, "—that new deputy you hired is sure enough one fast worker! Snake Dunkett was killed last night! In front of the Striped Tiger—and Kasta arrested Jeff Morris an' threw him in the can!"

Ten-Horse jumped his voice to Tabernacle Mountain. *"Hell's fire!"* he cried, and got out of his chair like its seat had burnt his trousers. "Never mind the grub," he said, and bolted for the door.

He dived from the porch and landed in his saddle. Fifty-eight seconds later he pulled up before the Sheriff's Office, slid to the ground, and strode grimly up the steps.

The unmelodious voice of the new deputy came through the window's broken glass in a yowl that sounded like a coyote's death-rattle.

With an oath Ten-Horse kicked open the door and strode inside.

Pony George sat on a corner of a badly-scarred desk, one leg crossed above the other, his pad settled on the knee of the topmost leg, and his pencil raised like the baton of a gay drum-major. He took one look at the sheriff's face and stopped with his mouth wide open.

"What the hell's goin' on round here?" Ten-Horse demanded.

"I—I—Why, I was just doin' a bit of work on

m' new ballad," George said innocently. "No harm in—"

Ten-Horse waved the words aside. "I ain't talkin' about that stuff," he growled, raking an irritable glance across the upset office. "I'm talkin' about Jeff Morris—one of the biggest gents in this part of the county! What in hell did you shove him in the cooler for?"

"Oh, him?" said Pony George indifferently. "Didn't yuh say if any of these hard-case hombres gave me any mouth, tuh slap 'em in the brisket an' shove 'em in the cooler till they sang a diff'rent tune? Thought yuh said a guy named Darst was bossin' this town. Well, I didn't bother *him!* All I did was—"

"I know what you did, all right!" Ten-Horse planted both brown fists upon his hips and glared. "You jailed the guy that controls more votes around this country than any three other gents put together! I—"

"You tol' me—"

"Yeah, I told you! But I expected you t' use some discretion!" Ten-Horse snarled, and sent another raking glance across the office. "What in thunder happened to this office? Don't tell me this is jest the result of your difference of opinion with Morris!"

"That guy! Well, I guess not!" George said emphatically. "He come like a lamb when I jabbed my hog-laig in his brisket—the way this office looks is on account of another guy. A gum-chawin', beetle-browed squirt in a boulder hat which claimed he was a dick from El Paso," George prevaricated. "He—"

"A dick! From El Paso?" Ten-Horse glowered accusingly. "What would a damn El Paso dick be doin' here, I'd like to know!"

"So would I! I ast him, an' when he started t' yank his smoke-pole, I took it away from him an' threw it out the winder. Then he jumped me. We had it hot an' heavy fer a spell. I sure thought I was a goner one time! He was smackin' me over the shoulders with that durn chair—but I got a-hold of his laig an' when I started chawin' on his ankle, he didn't lose no time in headin' fer other parts! Last I seen of 'im was a dustcloud in the distance."

Ten-Horse eyed him in some wonder. Apparently he could not make up his mind whether George was to be congratulated or called a plain damn liar. He looked again around the office, shook his head, and grunted: "Tell me about that killin' at the Striped Tiger—an' don't give me nothin' fancy. I want the unadulterated truth."

George regarded him reproachfully, chewed his lip and finally gave him all the particulars he possessed. "Snake Dunkett, I been told, was gnawin' the rag with three-four fellas out front of Morris' place. That stomp was goin' full blast inside. Dunkett was sayin' somethin' about some fella gettin' hung, when a guy in black clothes jogs up an' sits there eyin' him like he was somethin' the cat dragged in. Dunkett give the guy some lip, an' the fella jabbed 'im with his knife an' rode off laffin'. 'F yuh kin make any sense outen it, yuh're a smarter bird than I be."

"Talkin' 'bout some fella gettin' hung, eh?" mused Ten-Horse speculatively. "Didn't put no name to the fella, did he?"

"I reckon he did, but I don't remember. Them fellas I was questionin' was some mixed up in their accounts."

"No doubt," said Ten-Horse dryly. "Well, where's the knife?"

Pony George's voice became a deal less confident. "I'd like tuh know myself," he growled, and looked at the sheriff covertly. What he saw did not reassure him. He said hurriedly: "It was a reg'lar Arkinsaw toothpick, from all accounts, an'—"

"Oh!" said Ten-Horse coldly. "You let the murderer get away, an' you let the knife get away—"

"Wal, gallivantin' grapes!" snarled George. "The damn blade was gone before I got there, an' as fer—"

"Who was first to touch the body?" Jones demanded.

"S'far as I could find out, it was Darst."

George relaxed a little when he saw the way

Ten-Horse took that name. He commenced a rummaging through his pockets and, finally, with a sigh he brought them both out empty. "You ain't got no Durham, hev yuh? I'm sure dyin' fer a smoke."

"Here," Jones said, and tossed his sack. "Leave a little for the next time."

George sniffed. "There must be somethin' about a sheriff's job," he muttered, "that makes gents parsimonious. I never seen such tightwads with terbacca as you an' Red an' Anders. Now if *I* was makin' the han'some salary you are, I'd present yuh with a carton. I'd—"

"For the love of Mike, dry up an' give me a chance t' think," growled Ten-Horse irritably. "You oughta rent your gab to a windmill!"

But Pony George was not offended. "Some guys," he said, "would give their pants tuh be able tuh talk like me."

There is no telling what Ten-Horse might have answered, for at that moment the door shoved open and a runty puncher bow-legged in. He stared around with an open curiosity. "Looks like a Kansas twister'd struck this place. What yuh been doin'—arguin'?"

"What do you want, Shorty?" Jones said.

The newcomer looked at him resentfully. "Well, yuh ain't *obliged* t' listen. But I rode in t' tell yuh that they hanged Ol' Man Hart yesterday evenin'—"

"Who did!" Ten-Horse burst out furiously. "Where?"

"Over by Syler's Park." Shorty Hebron grinned a little, fatuously. "I ain't tellin' *who*. But I'll say this much. They hung 'im fer a rustler. Found one o' them brass tags his chaps is decorated with over on the Bar X bedground, an' claimed he'd had a hand in spiritin' off two hundred head of Bar X beef which has turned up missin'."

"That's a helluva joke—"

"It ain't no joke—it's Gawd's truth as I'm standin' in these boots! An' don't let it out I told yuh!"

Ten-Horse got a cigar from his coat pocket and bit an end off viciously. "Humph!" he said at last, scratching a match to light it. "Don't see there's much I can do about it now. Why didn't you tell me this yesterday?"

"I was busy," Hebron answered sullenly.

"I was, too," Jones grunted with some sarcasm. "I was figurin' to attend that stomp las' night, but instead I had t' go out huntin' that blasted Bloody-Runner. You're old enough t' realize duty should come first. If you know any more about this business than you've told, you better spill it."

"I said my piece," Hebron grunted. "Wild hawses won't git no more. *I* don't wanta turn up some mornin' hangin' to no limb!"

"Does Slow Jim know?"

"Sure he knows! I told him soon's I'd found it

out. I saw 'em at it an' went fer him right off—"

"You saw the lynchers, did you?"

Hebron paled as he realized the brash admission he had made. "Ten-Hawse, fer Gawd's sake don't let this get around! My life wouldn't be worth a plugged nickel," he whined. "Them birds would snuff me like a candle!"

"I'll keep the fact in mind. Looks like, though, you might's well spill the rest now. I've got to do somethin' about this, an' I can't do much blind."

Hebron shook his head stubbornly. "Nothin' doin'. I said too much a'ready. 'F I'd had the sense of a catbird I wouldn't 'a' told yuh nothin'."

Ten-Horse shifted ground. "What did Slow Jim say when you told him?"

Hebron's mouth curled scornfully. "He 'lowed he was pullin' out."

"Pullin' out? Why, he can't do that! He's got more interest in this thing than *I* have! It's *his ol' man!*"

" 'S what I told him. But he said one death in the Hart fambly was plenty. He ain't got no guts."

Ten-Horse frowned. "Go easy, Mister. Slow Jim used t' to be my pard, an' I ain't lettin' no gent cast them kind of slurs. You talk careful if you place any value on your hide."

"Well, it's the code, ain't it?"

"Mebbeso. But Slow Jim's prob'ly got his reasons."

"Well, if it was *my* ol' man I'd sure do somethin'

42

about it!" Hebron stated. "What'll Tony say about him layin' down that way?"

"Oh!" Ten-Horse said, and frowned. He stood that way awhile, leaning against the wall and staring thoughtfully at nothing. "I reckon that explains it," he murmured.

He looked up a little grimly. "Well," he said, "George will go over there with you. Old Hart'll have to be cut down—"

George said reproachfully: "I don't see why you can't go with 'im. *I* ain't lost no corpses, an' besides—"

"You ain't lost your job, yet, either," Jones said coldly. "But you might if I decide I can get along without you."

"Oh, all right," George growled grumpily. "If yuh're goin' tuh take that attitude, I'll go. But I don't like it." He looked unhappily at Hebron. "When you figger t' go—tomorrow?"

Ten-Horse said: "You'll go right now *an' like it!*"

"Anyways," George argued, "I don't see why yuh can't go with us."

"Because I got to apologize for you to Morris, an' let him out of jail. An' after that I want to take a look at Dunkett. An' then I'm figurin' to feed my face an' have a talk with Darst. In plain words, I'm goin' to be b-u-s-y—busy! Now get on your way, an' keep in mind I want Hart's body brought to town."

VI

Deuces Darst Pulls in His Breath

"Stopped beatin' your wife yet?" Ten-Horse hailed.

Oaths and maledictions poured from the region of Jeff Morris' cell in a violent, all-engulfing wave. It sounded like the man was on the verge of apoplexy.

"Tck, tck, tck!" Jones raised a cautioning hand. "Look out or you'll wake up the baby—Good grief, you're all swelled up like a carbuncle! Take it *easy* now, Mister Morris. Lean back careful an' relax. Remember your blood pressure!"

"You let me outa this goddam jail!" roared Morris furiously. "I'll hev your badge for this if it's the last damn' thing I do! I'll—"

"Now, now, sir—*please!* I understand just how you feel," Ten-Horse told him soothingly. "But it's all been a terrible mistake. Workin' yourself up like that'll be sure t' give you indigestion. You must relax—just set back an' take a long, deep breath. Count ten—count a hundred. Like I said, it was all a mistake. Some damn fool tol' my deputy you was beatin' yo' wife—"

"That deputy!" Morris swore. "I'm goin' t' beat that deputy up so bad his folks won't know him

44

from a fresh hide! I'm goin' t' bat his head down round his neck like a collar! I'm goin'—"

"Sure you are," Jones interrupted placatingly. "I'm going to let you out in jest a minute. I come down here soon's I heard about it—could any gent 'a' done more? It was on account I been out chasin' that dang Bloody-Runner that this was allowed t' happen. My—"

"Don't stand there handin' me that slush!" Morris howled. "Get them damn' keys an' git me outa here! By God, I'll—"

"But look," Jones wheedled. "Don't take it out on my new deputy. I know he's dumber than a ox—that fella don't know a B from a bull's foot! But I gotta have some help. *He* didn't know who you was! He don't know a soul this side of Pecos. 'Course, if he had known you and Darst was pard—"

"*Will you shut up?* I want out of here—*an' right damn now!*"

In this dim light, Morris' eyes glowed like chunks of blast-furnace coal. His voice was hoarse with frenzy. It long had been his boast he'd never been inside a jail and never would be; and the thought of the town's very probable reaction to his arrest was filling his soul with a chagrin only known to the politically powerful. He was all but frothing at the mouth—as Jones could see.

Jones said: "Do take it easy, sir. I'll see that

George makes a public apology an' that you are ful—"

"I don't want no *'pology!*" Morris snarled. "I wanta git *outa* here! If you don't unlock this—"

"All right, all right, all *right!*" Ten-Horse said. "I'm unlockin' it fast as I can, ain't I? D'you think this key's Aladdin's Lamp? Keep yo' gosh-blamed trousers on!"

He swung the cell door open and Morris came stalking forth like an enraged cat. He looked—as Ten-Horse later confided to the black-haired biscuit-shooter—"about as ugly as galvanized sin!"

"Where's my gun?" he demanded thickly. "An' my billfold? An' the loose change that pussy-faced hyena lifted from my pockets? Give 'em to me—*quick!* I'm goin' to—"

"You know," Ten-Horse cut through his tirade thoughtfully, "you ain't doin' yourself a bit of good with that there brand of talk. Sounds more like to me you oughta be put in a lunatic asylum than left free to roam the public streets." He squinted up his eyes and surveyed the saloon-man frowningly.

"I'm givin' you your gun an' money, an' I'm lettin' you go. But I'm givin' you warnin' here an' now. You leave that deputy plumb alone or I'll be riddin' you of your leaf-lard permanent—*savvy?*"

"You—I—you—" Morris spluttered. "I'll make you wish you'd never been born! I'll—"

"Yeah; you'll shout, too," Ten-Horse grinned.

• • •

After Morris with a malignant scowl had departed, the gaunt and yellow-haired sheriff of Hudspeth County tramped over to the nearest hash-house and surrounded his long-delayed nourishment.

It was dark by the time he left the restaurant. He turned a quick gaze up and down the street, then sauntered toward the coroner's.

There was a light burning in that gentleman's house. Ten-Horse knocked with the noise of the law and, without waiting for an answer, shoved the door open and strode inside.

The door opened onto a combination living room and office. Dunkett's body occupied a couch in the corner and Doc Millbane, the Coroner, sat beside it with a week-old newspaper. He looked up with a grunt as Ten-Horse entered.

"Thought it was you," he remarked. "Nobody else would bang a door like that, an' if they had they'd of waited for an invite before they come barging in."

Ten-Horse said: "Let's have the real lowdown on Dunkett. Was he killed by a knife or wasn't he?"

Doc Millbane, a serious man habitually dressed in black, tall and stooped and with a pair of steel spectacles eternally parked on his longish nose, nodded emphatically. "He certainly was, Andrew! A sharp and heavy one, by the look of the wound. Must have entered the—"

"Never mind all that," Jones interrupted. "If you say it was a knife, that settles it s' far as I'm concerned. Much obliged. I gotta be amblin' on."

And he went forthwith.

It seemed a heap like George's information was plumb accurate. But a fellow never knew. It was always best to check these things. And right now he had a burning hunch Darst hadn't reached Dunkett's body first by accident. Darst didn't do things by accident.

Ten-Horse rapped one of his loud knocks on the outside door of the Striped Tiger's private back room. Darst's careful voice said, "Who's there?"

"The Sheriff of Hudspeth County," Ten-Horse stated definitely. "Open up."

A key grated in the lock and the door swung inward several cautious inches.

"C'mon," Ten-Horse growled. "Wash off that war-paint an' let me in."

As though at last convinced that it was indeed the sheriff, Darst pulled open the door and Ten-Horse entered. He watched the gambler close and bolt the door behind him.

Darst flipped an expressive hand toward a chair. "Well," he said when Ten-Horse made no move to fill it, "what beneficent god do I owe this pleasure to?" Then his eyes grew hard and he dropped all pretense. "Cut it short, Jones. I got a poker game slated to start in here inside the next five minutes."

"Poker," Ten-Horse drawled, "is my favorite fruit." His gaze probed the gambler's expressionless face. "Where's that knife?"

Silently the gambler handed the weapon over. It was a Bowie, indistinguishable from hundreds of others save for the brand that was burned in the haft. Circle Bar.

Ten-Horse looked up. "Well?" His glance was sharp.

"That knife," Darst told him slowly, "belongs to Slow Jim Hart."

Ten-Horse knew it and hated it. He nodded reluctant agreement. There could be no doubt about the ownership of that blade. More times than he cared to recall, he had seen it strapped to Slow Jim's belt.

At last, with a shrug, he dismissed his frown. "I hear," he told the gambler, "that Tucker Hart was hung last night. What do you know about it?"

"Me?" Darst's hooded eyes revealed no emotion save a cold amazement. "I don't know anything about it, except that I understand Dunkett was sayin' something to that effect just before his light was snuffed. What were you *expecting* me to know?"

A slow light burned in Jones' pale eyes. His mouth-corners showed a faint, derisive curling. "Cautious Deuces Darst," he murmured. "Do you reckon," he asked reflectively, "that quarrel over fences an' water rights Hart was havin' with Sumptor could of had anything to do with it?"

"I wouldn't know," Darst said. "Personally, I've always found it wise to mind my own business and leave the other fellow to tend to his." There was a look about his highboned face inscrutable as a ledge of flint. "I believe Dunkett claimed that Hart was hung for rustling . . . something to do with two hundred Bar X beeves, I understand."

"Yeah, you understand, all right," Ten-Horse grunted coldly. "Time I get through with this business, I'm goin' to be doin' some understandin', too."

He had never liked the man and had taken scant pains to conceal the fact. Darst was a tinhorn and a puller-of-strings. According to some poor losers he was something else, as well, and 'had left his mother's wigwam in such a hurry he'd forgotten to bring his breech-clout.'

Ten-Horse eyed him meaningly. He said, "I'm takin' this knife along for evidence—an' safe-keeping."

Darst's strange face showed a thin and watchful smiling. "Sure," he said. "Good night."

Left alone, Darst took a tiny bit of pasteboard from a flowered vest pocket. In the lamp's pale light he closely scanned its penciled scrawl.

"The least shall be first. Let the greater culprits take heed and ponder the ways of Fate. Death rides the range."

The only signature was the crude sketch of a miniature black horseman. The symbol used by the Bandit of Bloody Run.

Sitting there, brooding over the strange message he had found impaled upon the knife, and over the sketch of that black horseman that had been used to sign the thing, the lamp's yellow flame cast a sinister network of light and shadow across Darst's angular features.

At last he roused himself and with an oath tore the pasteboard into bits. Dropping these into a capacious pocket of his black frock coat, he donned his hat, unbolted the door, and stepped into the blackness of the alley—to stop abruptly with indrawn breath.

VII

Ten-Horse Talks Cold Turkey

The silhouetted figure of a man cast a denser shape against the flowing shadows of this alley's gloom. A still, lank figure, whose edgy pose threw off an air of menace.

Darst stood rooted by the door, his upper body

tilted a little forward, his lean right hand rigidly spread above his gun. Something in the darkness of that yonder form clicked over a sudden thought in the gambler's mind. His spread hand dropped a little lower.

He said wickedly: "Well?"

The silhouette spoke. "That you, Deuces?"

A chill of fear ran a cold wave across the gambler's frame. He knew that voice. Too well. It was the voice of Slow Jim Hart.

And now Hart was moving forward. Lamplight, spilling from the unshaded office window, showed his face composed in lines of mastered calm. It was not at all the sort of expression Darst had been expecting. It puzzled him and put a keener glint in the alertness of his gaze.

Slow Jim murmured, "Howdy. Just comin' in to have a word with you. Not too busy, are you?"

"No busier than usual, I reckon. Come in." Darst stood aside.

Hart entered. Darst, following, kicked the door shut with his heel. He sat down watchful and reserved in a chair before his desk. Hart dropped into one nearby and stretched his legs before him, staring thoughtfully at his dusty boots.

The silence began to get uneasy.

Slow Jim's abruptly upraised glance did nothing to ease the situation.

Darst said at last, "What's on yore mind?"

"Several things," Hart answered slowly. "My

Dad's been hanged, Darst. Know anything about it?"

"No." The gambler's face was like a mask hacked out of wood. "Did you think I did?"

"I was just wonderin'. Darst," Slow Jim's voice grew strangely soft, "I been told Snake Dunkett was rubbed out last night. If so, it'll be the first of a damned bad breed."

No change could be detected on the gambler's high-boned face. He met Hart's probing stare without the twitching of a nostril. "Dunkett's dead, yes. He was knifed. . . . I got the note."

"Note?" Hart's eyes widened. "What note is that?"

Darst's watchful gaze was very bright. "The note that was on that knife."

Slow Jim let out his breath. " 'Fraid that's lost on me. I never was much good at riddles. You better chew it a little finer. What was in the note?"

Darst, alert and ready, told him.

But Slow Jim's face stayed blank.

A clever actor, Darst decided. Or did he, after all, know anything about that note? Someone else *could* have written it; Darst was not familiar with Hart's handwriting. Someone else *might* have driven that blade. But it was Darst's considered opinion that Hart was the author both of the note and Dunkett's death-thrust.

A deep man, Slow Jim. In many ways he resembled his hardbitten sire.

The gambler put on an air of affability. "What was it you wanted to see me about?"

Slow Jim rose. "I come by to tell you I'm gettin' out of the country. For the time bein', anyway. My Dad was framed, an' it strikes me if I stick around the same thing might happen to me."

"So you're pullin' out, eh?" Darst fiddled with his coat lapels and stared thoughtfully at the floor. "It might be the answer at that. I expect you're doin' a wise thing, Hart."

"That's the way I look at it."

"You're sellin' out, then?"

"I guess I better if I aim to keep on bein' healthy."

The gambler nodded. "We'll be sorry to see you go. But I can't say but what you're doin' the right thing."

"I think so. You see, Deuces, I been sparkin' Tony Sumptor quite a spell. Fact is, we're just about engaged. Seems like it might be a bit more pleasant if we started housekeepin' in some other state. There's no love lost between her ol' man an' me, I guess you know. Won't have me around the place. I'll get located somewhere an' then send back for Tony."

"I see," Darst said in a perfectly expressionless voice. "Yeah, I guess you got the right idea."

But when Slow Jim had gone, Darst leaned forward and blew out the light. Then, under cover of the darkness, his long-masked features gave way to an expression of wildest rage.

● ● ●

Ten-Horse was just putting the finishing touches to his job of cleaning up the Sheriff's Office when the door shoved open and Slow Jim Hart stepped in.

"Howdy, Ten-Horse."

"Hullo, yourself," the sheriff said, and gave his visitor a long and careful stare. "You're lookin' kinda peaked round the gills," he observed. "Like mebbe your supper wasn't settin' well. What's up?"

"You heard about that hangin'?"

"Sure. You come in after cartridges?"

Slow Jim chewed his lip. He looked uneasy.

"Jumpin' Jerrycows," Ten-Horse growled; "you don't need t' be afeard of *me!* Ain't we been pardners? 'F there's anything I can do, sing out. Needin' money? I ain't got much, but you're welcome to what there is."

Slow Jim didn't answer. He just stood there fingering his gunbelt and looking more and more uncomfortable. "Tell me," he finally blurted, "what you think about that lynchin'."

"I ain't doin' any thinkin' till I find out all the facts." Ten-Horse's eyes held a faint and lazy gleaming. "But you don't need to let that hold *you* back."

"Not aimin' to—I'm pullin' out."

"You're *what?*" Ten-Horse stared incredulously. Then a wide grin broke across his features. "Oh," he said; "I see."

"I guess you don't. I'm serious," Slow Jim said

55

a little hoarsely. "I'm gettin' out of this damn country."

"Gettin' out! What for?"

Slow Jim made a weary gesture. "My Dad was framed, Ten-Horse. Way I look at it, one death in the Hart family's a-plenty. I—"

"Then you better look again. I reckon you need spectacles," Ten-Horse muttered. "By gee, I used t' think you was a *man!* What's happened to your spinal column?"

Slow Jim flushed and eyed the floor. Then his eyes came up defiantly. "I don't see no call to hang around an' get my own self killed! I'm engaged t' marry Tony Sumptor an'—"

"Does she know about this idee? What's she think about you crawlin' off to hunt a hole? I'll bet she feels real proud o' you!"

"She don't know about it yet. I haven't had a chance to get over there. That's where you—"

"Don't count me in on anything like that!"

"Come out of the dark ages," Slow Jim growled, a darkness in his cheeks. "We're livin' in another century. People don't go round gunnin' for each other any more! Texas is gettin' civilized now, an'—"

"Oh, is that so? Excuse *me,*" Ten-Horse bowed. "Way they hung your Dad, I thought I must be livin' in Kaintucky—"

"That's what the matter is with you!" Hart broke in hotly. "You still got that country in your system! Just 'cause you was foaled by a fightin' family out of that country's feudin'est county, you figure every time some hellion does a fella dirt, he oughta hang a gun on his hip an' go out an' do some killin'! Well, I can't see it that way. An' what's more, I ain't allowin' to do it!"

"If you don't give a damn about your ol' man," Ten-Horse scowled, "by gee, you ought to have some regard for the traditions of this country. A eye for a eye—you know the code. An' I'll bet my boots you know who's responsible for that lynchin', too!"

Slow Jim waved the words aside. "You might as well let up. I know where my responsibilities lie. I figure on marryin' Tony Sumptor. I'm goin' to advertize the ranch for sale an' go hunt up a peaceful climate. 'F I can get far enough away, mebbe we'll stand a halfway chance to *enjoy* our married life!"

"You handed her all these idees yet?"

"That's what I dropped in about. As my best friend in this region, I figured you'd naturally explain it to her for me. I'd stick around here if I thought it would do any good. But I don't; I know this mess will never get itself ironed out as long as there's a Hart in this locality.

"Now, I want you to do this for me, pardner. I want you to ride out to the Lazy D an' get Antonia off to one side. Tell her what I'm up to. Show her how my way is best, an' why. Explain that if I—

Well, I'll leave the details up to you. Tell her I'll be sendin' for her soon's I get somethin' lined up —it won't be long. I know cattle an' I know ranchin'. I'd go out there an' tell her myself, but her ol' man don't like me an' there'd be no sense'n gettin' him all riled up."

He looked at Ten-Horse anxiously. "You'll do this for me, won't you, pardner?"

"Is it the way you're standin' makes you look so much like a screwball?" Ten-Horse asked.

Slow Jim's face went red and white. He seemed to hold himself with an effort. It looked for a minute as though he meant to strike Ten-Horse. Then some of the smoke went out of his eyes and he put a hand to the door.

"Leastways, you'll look after her for me, won't you?"

Ten-Horse eyed him coldly. "I'll be lookin' after her," he said; "but it sure won't be for you!"

For long moments after Slow Jim had gone, Ten-Horse sat at his desk with his chin cupped in his hands and a light of bitter brooding in his eyes. He recalled now Hebron's words. "No guts!" the puncher had told him sneeringly. And it sure looked like fitting Slow Jim's case.

In the years that he had known Slow Jim, in the years that they'd been wild young fools and sowing their oats together, Slow Jim, he was recalling, had always been a little odd. Always a man to start a thing, but never the man to finish it. He'd often made loud talk before tough hombres. But when it had looked like gun-jerking time, he'd always found an interest someplace else. Of course, he *was* a little slow—the nickname hadn't been hung on him for nothing. But any man with a fleck of iron in his veins, it was Ten-Horse's unconditional opinion, would not be leaving a country that had killed his Dad—not without doing something about it first.

He looked up, shaking off his brooding thoughts, as the clump of booted feet rang echoes from the walk outside. The door swung open then and Bill McCash strode in, smacking dust from his trail-grimed clothing.

McCash had the slouch that is common to Texans, but it did not go with his look. He was lean, with a suggestion of panther grace in the flowing smoothness of his movements. A dark, blunt man with a lean-carved face and striking profile. He had a bold glance that more than matched his manner, and held a high opinion of himself that was manifest in all his acts.

"Well," he said with a scowl, "what did that pussy-footin' Hart hombre want with you? Been swearin' out a warrant?"

"He wasn't swearin' out no warrant here. Was you expectin' him to?"

"I wouldn't put it past him. His kind of worm take their troubles to the law." McCash's lips curled. "I served notice on him to stay away from Tony Sumptor—her ol' man's some particular who she does her gallivantin' with. So's Hart would know I wasn't peddlin' no damn loads, I tapped my gun when I told him. An' he sure absorbed my point o' view. Thought mebbe he'd come over here hopin' t' sick you onto me."

Ten-Horse looked him over unfavorably. Like a lot of others, he'd never cared a heap for Bill. McCash was a deal too cocky for his taste.

"You can rest easy," Ten-Horse told him. "I don't make a practice of goin' round fightin' other folks' battles for 'em. I got plenty worries of my own."

McCash drawled, "I'm plumb relieved t' hear you say so. Kinda had me worried." His full red lips stretched out in a cynical curve that Ten-Horse ignored. "You caught that stagecoach robber yet?"

"Not yet—but I allow I'll get him soon."

"You an' that Hart pussy-footer," McCash sneered, "make a pair to draw to. Only trouble is, a man'd have a hard time drawin' enough t' git you outa the four-flusher class."

Ten-Horse cuffed his black hat in a tall piratical slant. He let the crack go by, remembering the Golden Rule. But his narrowed eyes showed a steely gleam.

McCash's vanity would not leave it there.

Shoving free of his lounging place against the

wall, he opened the door. "I find it hard," he sneered, "judgin' between you blow-shoots. But I guess your tripe's been pickled, 'cause it sure takes picklin' t' stomach pardnerin' round with a louse like Hart."

"You may be right," said Ten-Horse softly. "But you better be careful, or some o' this picklin'll be takin' you 'longside the jaw."

Bill McCash laughed. "I've quit readin' fairy tales."

He made as though to go. Then his head wheeled round for a final admonition. "You tell that fool t' stay away from my girl. Tell him I'll shoot on sight—not that it'll ever be necessary. That guy ain't got enough sand t' clog the eye of a *needle!*"

"You've said enough," grunted Ten-Horse, and put his fist against McCash's tough face with a force that put him through the door. His bootheel caught on an upraised plank and he sat down hard in the dusty street.

Like that he sat, with his features a study in stunned amazement. Knowledge of who and where he was abruptly darkened his face like a thunder-cloud. He came off the ground with a thin-lipped curse and drove a hand at his groin.

But the hand never touched his weapon. It stopped two inches short and breath leaped into him shrilly. His wide eyes goggled like a cat-scared sparrow's. For Ten-Horse had followed him out. And now that gentleman's heavy gun was grimly prodding his belly.

The look in Jones' cold eyes warned that little inducement was needed to set that gun a-spouting.

"Hold on," Bill cried; "I'll take that back!"

"Yes, you swivel-eyed polecat! You're daw-gone right you will!" The tight grin on Ten-Horse's lips was like a shouted warning. "I'm tellin' you flat an' it goes like it lays; you keep outa my game, or—"

And he turned on his heel, going back into the office without bothering to list the consequences.

VIII

"You Better Not Play Round Doris May"

Pony George, in the shank of night, returned to Eagle Flat sans escort; glad, if the truth be known, to shake loose of the unprepossessing Shorty Hebron, who had talked of funereal subjects from the time they left town until George had disgustedly told him to 'go on home an' give yore jaw a rest.'

The bulk of Eagle Flat's main drag was buried in Old Man Night's hip pocket as George urged his limping crowbait past the baleful lights of the Striped Tiger and headed for the Sheriff's Office.

Lampglow, spilling across the plank walk before

the Alamo Restaurant, turned the deputy's thoughts toward food and he swung abruptly from his mount, threw down its reins, and clumped inside, taking a stool at the empty counter.

"Great guns, gal," he exclaimed as the black-haired biscuit-shooter stepped forward to serve him, "don't you never rest?"

"Sure," she said, "but on Wednesday nights I work. The boss has to get off sometime, and on Wednesday nights he drops his profits on Jeff Morris' poker tables."

"That guy," declared George, meaning Morris, "is a public nuisance. Thinks he owns this burg lock, stock, an' barrel. He don't scare me none, though! Juh hear about me lockin' 'im up?"

"As conversational fodder that story's a thing to date time by," she told him, grinning. "What'll you have? We got—"

"Cup o' cawffee, stack o' wheat, an' plenty of syrup," George stated. "An' a slab of Dutch apple pie t' top 'er off." He looked at her slanchways. "Care tuh join me?"

" 'Fraid the boss won't stand for it," she murmured regretfully. "But I'll tell you what—" she smiled, "I'll loaf around out front here while you're eating and chew the rag. How's that?"

"Peaches an' cream," George chuckled. "I sure need inspiration. I'm writin' a new ballad. It's called 'The Bandit of Bloody Run'—how's that fer a title?"

The black-haired biscuit-shooter paled a bit and stopped swabbing the counter. "Fine," she said hurriedly. "I'll go tend your order."

And off she went.

George looked after her with a frown. "Now what in thunder's the matter with her?" he muttered. "Yuh'd think I'd tromped on 'er pet corn, way she went prancin' outa here." A light of speculation chased the scowl from his dried-apple countenance as he gazed at the door that had closed behind her. "Sure is pow'ful easy on the eyes, though. I'll hev tuh know her better."

She was back in a moment with his food. After arranging it before him, she leaned close a moment and, with a swift glance in either direction, whispered: "You wanta be careful how you sling that gunman's name around."

"Who yuh torkin' about?" George asked. "That Morris pelican? Why, I kin whip that whoppy-jawed chipmunk with both fists lashed b'hind m' back an' one laig broke! I ain't escared of *him!*"

"I mean the Bandit," she declared. "He's killed four men now since he opened up operations. It wouldn't surprise *me* none," she added, "if it comes out he had a hand in hangin' Ol' Man Hart!"

But George just sniffed. Dead men didn't interest him. "Le's tork about somethin' more cheerful—you, fer instance. What'd yo' mother call yuh?"

"Doris," said the biscuit-shooter smiling. "Doris

64

May Lee—but no relation to that rowdy that runs the Bar X ranch. *My* folks had a pedigree that run clear back to the Mayflower!"

"Wal, good fer them!" George approved, beaming. "My ol' man allus claimed there was consid'able hist'ry back o' *us*. I pers'nally, though, don't hold with ancestor worship. Kings an' queens never put no butter on *my* bread!" He waved his coffee cup vehemently. "It's the man hisself what counts! If a fella's got the goods he kin get along. Now, take my poetry—"

"Here," she said, "drink your coffee."

"Y'betcha!"

He picked up his coffee cup and took a big swig. His eyes got big as saucepans and his cheeks bulged like a woodchuck's. His face was red as fire.

Doris May's face showed alarm. She leaned forward anxiously. "Whatever is the matter?" she exclaimed.

George put down the cup and gingerly felt it with his other hand. He swallowed manfully and mopped his sweating forehead, blowing a gusty breath at the ceiling's smoke-streaked beams. He cast a jaundiced eye at the steaming cup. "Black as sin, hot as love, an' stronger'n the Devil beatin' tanbark!—just," he added hurriedly, "the way I like it!"

George climbed down from his decrepit nag before the Sheriff's Office and went inside. As he'd been coming up the street, he had heard some horseman go racking out of town. Now, seeing Ten-Horse all hunched up by his desk, scowling and cleaning his guns, George put two and two together, finally arriving at four.

"Wal," he said, "who was the departin' guest? He sure lit outen here like he was mad 'nough t' swaller the Devil with his horns on! Shake loose, my fine-feathered friend; who was he?"

"Bill McCash—the mutton-faced Mormon sidewinder! I'll bet he don't come struttin' round *here* no more. I sure put *him* in his place! An' he better stay there, too. Next time I'm like t' use a gun."

"Holy smoke!" George said, and whistled. "What did the knothead do?"

"Never mind," Ten-Horse told him grumpily. "Where's Hart's body?"

"Dead an' buried, my friend," Pony George said loftily. "I sent that Hebron pelican back tuh Momma—cripes, that guy is cheerful as a crutch!"

Ten-Horse glowered. "Thought I told you to bring Hart's body back t' town! What'd you want t' go an' bury—"

"Say, listen! Quit pickin' on me, can't yuh? *I* didn't bury *no one*—Hart was cut down an' planted 'fore we got there. Yuh could see by the rope how some'un had cut 'im down. We found the grave clost by. Couldn't see no use in diggin' 'im up ag'in. Leave 'im rest."

66

Ten-Horse was frowning thoughtfully. At last he looked up, running a lean brown hand through his hair. "Slow Jim, I guess," he muttered. Then he looked at Pony George. "You stick around town—you can turn in, if you want to. I'm goin' t' take a little pasear aroun' the country. Don't count on me for nothing till you see me. I may be gone a couple days."

"*Vaya con Dios*," George murmured airily. "Oh, say—yuh wanta hear m' ballad about the Bandit 'fore yuh go?"

"I'm too busy to be foolin' round with that stuff—"

"Wal, fer cryin' out loud! An' here I been figgerin' yuh was a man of some discernment! You can sniff if yuh want to, but Doris May likes it—"

"What does that pearl-diver know about judgin' poetry?"

"Yuh needn't go throwin' down on Doris May," George said indignantly. "Some of the greatest women in hist'ry has washed dishes—she's got a pedigree longer than yore arm! Her father was Captain of the Mayflower—"

Ten-Horse turned around. "You talking about that black-haired waitress over at the Alamo hash-house?"

"I sure am! An' she ain't no lousy dish-washer, neither! She's a biscuit-shooter—an' a dang good 'un! I'll thank yuh to remember it."

"A biscuit-shooter, eh? Well, she may be one at that, but her coffee—"

"Say no more," George interrupted hastily. "I know all about her cawffee."

"That stuff she serves," Ten-Horse insisted doggedly, "has been warmed up for anyways two months. I drank some when they first went into business—her ol' man runs the joint. They color it with shoe-black."

George sighed. "Wal," he pointed out, "she's a durn nice gal, an' purty as a li'l red wagon. Her teeth—"

Ten-Horse looked him over appraisingly. "I wish you all the luck," he said gravely. "Can't quite figure out, though, what you'll do for money when the pair of you get hitched up. There's a mortgage plastered on that place an' her ol' man ain't got no use fer married women—"

"Here—hold on, there!" George said, blinking. "Hitched up? Why, hell! I got no idear o' marryin' her! Where'd yuh git that crazy notion? Love 'em an' leave 'em's allus been my motter!"

"Then you better not play round Doris May. Her father was a ol' time vigilante. An' he's kep' good care of his shotgun."

Grinning, Ten-Horse left the office.

Five minutes later he swung aboard his barrel-gutted bronc, Stovepipe, and, hazing his other nine horses ahead of him, rode off up the Killbone Canyon in the direction of Lee's Bar X.

IX

The End of a Perfect Day

After Jones had gone, Pony George looked kind of glum till he noticed how Ten-Horse had cleaned up the office. He saw that Ten-Horse had got a new chair for his desk, too, and after a few minutes of rather morose silence he dropped into it wearily.

He glanced at the clock. One-thirty! "Great guns," he muttered. "High time all respectable people was a-bed. Guess I'll hit the hay. I reckon this office can take care of itself fer two-three hours anyhow."

He killed the light and slammed the door behind him. Climbing into his saddle, he rode down the murky street. There were no stars showing and the moon was a pale lopsided disc surrounded by a halo. He rode to the door of the livery stable and dismounted beneath its lantern, shaking the dozing attendant to disgruntled wakefulness.

"You the hostler?" George asked, poking him, "or jest somethin' the boss left here t' brace that door? Wal, come alive, then, fer gran'maw's sake! This bronc wants takin' care of; he's done a hard day's work. Give 'im a rubdown, put a blanket on him, an' see he gits a extry-large hatful of oats."

Still grumbling, the hostler got to his feet and stretched. He looked George's mount over skeptically. "Hell," he sneered, "that ain't no hawse! That's a annymated skeleton—a mem'ry! Cart it off; you can't leave that thing round here! What yuh tryin' t' do—scare our thoroughbreds?"

"Thoroughbreds!" George snorted. "I kin count the thoroughbreds round *this* stable on the finger of one hand! This is him," he stated, *"right here,"* and slapped his crowbait on the rump.

The ancient steed tottered round with a doleful groan and came to rest against the hostler. That gentleman made a fine upstanding leaning-post, and George's horse was quick to utilize it, relaxing with a sigh.

"Here—cut that out!" the hostler cried, bracing himself. He shaved with both his outthrust arms, finally getting the old plug on a strictly vertical basis. But the moment he stopped pushing the horse slopped right back at him.

As things sometimes do at most unlikely moments, a stone picked this precise instant to turn beneath the hostler's foot. With a curse he lost his balance and went down. And George's horse, giving an alarmed whinny, went down atop him.

George took one good look. "Shucks," he said. And, whistling vigorously, he set off down the road.

Breasting the Striped Tiger, he observed that

its lights were dimmed. "All gone home but the drunks," he muttered, "an' they'll be thrown out soon." He didn't bother going in, though Ten-Horse had made it plain he was expected to. "But not at this time o' night," George said. "I gotta git t' bed."

He turned into the hotel's dingy lobby, finding it deserted. One lamp, turned way down, burned palely. Leaning across the desk he reached up and got his key. Then he climbed the squeaking stairs, each step driving eerie sounds across the late hour's hush. Or, perhaps, George thought happily, it was that fellow down at the stable.

Minutes later, in his room and with half his clothes peeled off, George reached up to blow out the lamp.

The lamp went out, but not by George's agency. It was blown out for him with a tinkle of shattered glass by a slug that came within an ace of taking off the side of his head. And the report whose slamming echoes woke the night burst wickedly from the region of Jeff Morris' Striped Tiger Bar!

Chief Deputy Kasta of Hudspeth County waited not upon the order of his going, but grabbed up his clothes and fled at once—and felt no shame for his promptness!

X

Ten-Horse Does Some Thinking

It was nearly four o'clock when the Sheriff of Hudspeth County reached a place along the rim-rock where he could look down upon the rambling canyon housing the headquarters buildings of Kinch Lee's Bar X ranch. It was still dark, though, and no light showed from the canyon floor; all was black as a stack of stove-lids.

Ten-Horse hobbled out his ponies, dragged his saddle to a spot where the dwarf cedars' piney mat looked promising, put his head upon it and stretched his length out wearily.

But he was far from sleep, and knew it. His mind was far too active with the multiple problems forced upon him for any thoughts of sleep. He built himself a smoke left-handed and with a thumb-nail scratched a match to flame; cupping it guardedly lest some gent of uneasy conscience down below should happen to spy it.

Exhaling the fragrant smoke, he prepared to give considerable serious attention to the disturbing factors that had roused to plague his reign as 'boss' of Hudspeth County.

Who had participated in the lynching of Tucker

72

Hart? That, at the moment, appeared to be the vital problem. It wasn't, of course—he knew that. His main problem, as the County Commissioner had taken pains to show him, was the task of throwing a successful monkey wrench in the evil machinations of that hombre from Bloody Run. If he could catch and jail the gentleman, all would be well along the western front. But failing that . . . "You stop that fella, or else—" the County Commissioner had said. "We expect you either to kill the varmint outright or drive him from the county. If you can't do it, we'll get someone that can! The honor of this county is at stake!"

The path of a newly-elected sheriff, Ten-Horse reflected, more resembled prickly pear and wormwood than any bed of roses!

But he wasn't letting it get him down. He was a sight more worried over that business of Tucker Hart. He'd known Tucker a long time, and liked him. Tough and ranniky Old Hart had been, but after his fashion a pretty square shooter, and a gent to ride the river with.

First thing to find out, naturally, was who had it in for him. That looked all too easy. Hart had wired his springs since the drought, and Tumble-weed Sumptor's Lazy D cattle needed water. There was so much alkali in the waters of Sumptor's nearly-depleted tanks that if a man should wet his neckerchief in them, he'd have to take a hammer to get the wrinkles out once it dried.

Small wonder Sumptor's cattle were not over-fond of Sumptor's range. Who could blame them if they found the savory sweetness of Hart's springs more to their liking? Not Ten-Horse—and certainly not Sumptor.

On the other hand, Ten-Horse could not find it in him to censure Hart for having fenced his water when Sumptor's cattle had descended on it in such an avalanche as to threaten complete destruction of his graze.

It was a pretty pickle, and no mistake!

Now that the Harts were gone, however, and Slow Jim was putting the spread up for sale, likely enough things would be a deal different. Sumptor cattle could use Hart's water freely till a new owner took possession; perhaps, even then, Sumptor would manage to make some satis-factory arrangement.

But, certainly, Sumptor was the man who had most to gain by Tucker's death. They'd never been very friendly even before this trouble over fence and water. Hart's had been the biggest outfit; Ten-Horse was rather inclined to think there'd been some jealousy on Sumptor's part, though he had little to substantiate this notion.

And Lee, he thought abruptly; where did Lee fit into this picture of old Hart's hanging? It had been on the bedground of Lee's rustled Bar X herd that someone had found, or claimed to find, that brass tag off Tucker Hart's chaps. How much truth was in it? Ten-Horse wondered. And how much truth was there in that tale of the rustled Bar X beef?

Not that no rustling operations had been going on. There'd been more rustling round here lately than a fellow could shake a stick at. Most folks claimed the Bandit of Bloody Run was back of it; but he furnished all too good a target for the home stretch of other men's didoes. All this stuff that was going on could hardly be the work of one lone man. Ten-Horse strongly doubted that it was even the work of one gang.

There was too much deviltry afoot by far!

And that fool bandit, with his fancy get-up and Jesse James hold-ups, made an excellent scapegoat behind which any gent who cared to don a mask and wield a ready gun could hide. Whatever was wrong about this range was almost certain to be eventually traced directly to the energy of that rascal from Bloody Run.

So far as he knew personally, Ten-Horse decided, it was entirely possible that Kinch Lee hadn't lost any beeves at all. It sounded good—sounded even logical—and provided an excellent reason for ridding the country of Tucker Hart. And anyone else other folk might take a dislike to.

Nothing was certain save that Tucker Hart was dead.

At that point in his cogitations Ten-Horse recalled the knife Deuces Darst claimed to have pulled from the body of Snake Dunkett. He berated himself for not seeking to get some information out of Slow Jim concerning that fatal blade.

It struck him suddenly that a lot of people were going to feel darned certain Slow Jim had done Dunkett in.

It was not a pleasant thought.

When two men have pardnered around together the way he and Slow Jim had, it usually takes considerably more than a 'murder weapon' to break that friendship up.

Ten-Horse might suddenly become convinced that young Hart was made of shoddy stuff; that in a pinch, or a tight place like the one he now was in, Slow Jim did not measure man-size; that he had a wishbone where his backbone ought to be. But for another man to hold a like opinion and voice it in his presence, was something the angular Jones would not stand for one holy minute. He had shown it when he threw Bill McCash from the Sheriff's Office. Slow Jim was his pardner—no matter what his metal.

As a matter of fact, Ten-Horse was greatly disappointed in Slow Jim. It took a pretty poor specimen, was his considered opinion, to do what young Slow Jim was doing. A *man,* knowing the identities of those responsible for his father's death, would have sought them out and called them to account if it was the last thing he did on earth. No Westerner worthy of the name would allow his father's murderers to go their ways without reprisal while he slunk off some place to feather a love nest.

Why, what would Antonia think of the man when she heard the news? One thing was certain, Ten-Horse vowed; she'd never learn such disgraceful facts from him!

He wondered whether that knife he'd got from Darst was the actual blade pulled by the gambler from Dunkett's body. It didn't seem like a fellow who'd do as Slow Jim appeared bent on doing would have had the nerve to have tackled the gun-armed Dunkett with a knife. Knives were things associated by Ten-Horse with Mexicans. It seemed to him a deal more likely that some Mex with a grouch had shoved that blade in Dunkett's chest.

And yet . . . *A black-garbed horseman with eyes that glowed like coals!*

That would not have been his own description of a Mexican.

He recalled the slinky mariner in which the gambler had made off with the knife. "An'," Ten-Horse muttered irritably, "if I hadn't called 'im on it, nobody'd know even yet where the damn thing went!"

Why should Darst have taken the blade at all? And, since he *had* taken it, why give it up to the sheriff? He could easily have denied all knowledge of the thing. There was something in the woodpile whose aroma, he decided, was distinctly brown.

If only he could find some way of making Hebron talk! It was a cinch the puncher knew who'd hung Slow Jim's old man. Had probably told Slow Jim. Maybe Slow Jim had advised him to keep his mouth shut—maybe. Sheriff Jones thought not. He figured a jug of something or other ought to loosen Hebron's tongue. He resolved to experiment at the earliest opportunity.

But there was always Lee—and he'd be seeing Lee very shortly.

In the meantime it might be wise to indulge in forty winks. It would soon be getting light, for false dawn was due to hang its tricky shades across the east. There were some aspects of this sheriffing game that weren't half bad; *cowboys* rose at 4:00 a.m.—and it was 3:59 right now!

With a kind of grin, Ten-Horse wrapped himself in his Navajo blanket and, with his ten fast horses hobbled round him, and a coyote's early morning yammer to relieve the piled-up Texas silence, he beckoned the goddess of sleep.

XI

A Little Hard Luck

"I stopped by," said Ten-Horse, "to tell you that there'll be a inquest in town at ten sharp tomorrow mornin'. You'll be expected t' be on hand."

"Inquest, eh?" Kinch Lee's eyes were speculative. "An' what's with me it got to do?"

"You been losin' cattle, ain't you?"

"Sure I cattle been losin'—goddlemighty, yes! I lost the other beef two hundred nights! Right off my bedground stole! Another ruin like that will raid me!"

Ten-Horse regarded the Bar X owner curiously. He'd never had any dealings with the man and only knew him by repute. He was not a native of the country, but had come in about ten years ago and bought out Sillbarger, the man who had started the Bar X brand. It was said he got the spread for a song. Be that as it may, Ten-Horse was convinced the man knew cattle; since taking over, he'd built the Bar X into a first-class spread. He'd even brought in blooded bulls and graded his stock for fancy prices.

Tall and mackerel-eyed he was, with three big moles at his mouth's left corner which it was his habit to be eternally fingering. Big of bone, when he stood as he now was standing with his head thrust forward and his shoulders a little hunched, he bore in Ten-Horse's eyes a most remarkable resemblance to a buzzard. It was uncanny the way his great hooked nose, its pointed end curled down before his traplike mouth, accentuated this illusion.

But Lee was odd in many more ways than one. A noticeable peculiarity was the difference in his eyes—one was blue and the other brown. Too, he was more reticent than his impediment of speech accounted for; Jones had heard it rumored the man had been a gun fighter before settling down in this locality, and thought it not unlikely that he had been—the long tapering fingers of his usually gloved hands bore out the notion well. His impediment of speech was a habit of generally twisting his words around—a result, some said, of getting cured of the stutters too fast. It was a tax on other people's nerves to get his meaning straight.

"Yeah," said Ten-Horse smoothly, "I heard about your beef. Dunkett was pursuin' the subject when that fella snuffed his light." He leaned forward with a heightened interest. "How well do you know Darst?"

Ten-Horse knew that question was a boner quick as he got it out. Change ran over Kinch Lee's face like a curtain dropped, erasing all expression.

"I don't know him well at all," Lee said, and

dropped the subject. "You like this sheriffin' job?"

"Oh, so-so," Ten-Horse said. "Well, I reckon I better be siftin' along. Got to notify a bunch of other fellas 'bout that inquest. Ten o'clock, remember. Sharp."

He stepped up into the saddle.

Lee cleared his throat. "'Fraid I won't be able to get to inquest for that town. Too much work t' do. Got my rustlers out after them boys, you know, an'—"

"Better let things slide here for a while. That inquest's apt to be a heap important—particular," Ten-Horse said with deceptive smoothness, "to them fellas that don't show up." He looked at the Bar X owner meaningly. "If you ain't there I'll have to send a deputy after you."

Kinch Lee stared. "Like that, eh?"

"This is murder, Lee—"

"Murder? When Dunkett was drivin' lead from his cutter?" Lee's eyebrows rose satirically.

Ten-Horse nodded. "The day of the Injun's past. The Law calls duelin' murder, Lee. You better be on hand."

"Listen," Lee said harshly. "I wasn't even in town when it happened. What the hell inquest would I be at your good?"

Ten-Horse squinted. "Chew that a little finer, will you?"

Lee's dark face showed color. His effort to keep his words straight whipped out veins along

81

his forehead. "When Dunkett got his light blowed, I was home here in the house—"

"Got proof of that fact, have you?"

Lee scowled. His left hand dropped a little closer to the pistol at his belt. "You callin' me a liar?"

"Not at all. I'm only askin' what a judge would ask in my place."

The Bar X owner sneered. " 'F I was you I'd leave the judge's work for the judge. You might job him out of a get." His eyes showed a sulky brilliance. "You ain't told me yet why I have to tend that inquest."

"That," said Jones, "is the reason—because I *told* you to."

"Another week at this sheriffin'," Ten-Horse muttered, "an' I'll be 'bout as popular round this climate as a wet hound at a parlor social!"

He put his horses across a rise, swearing at them and snapping the blacksnake whip he carried. Down yonder was Eagle Flat and he was anxious to get there, having a number of things on his mind. Besides Kinch Lee, he'd seen a number of other ranchers. He had not, however, gone near the Lazy D. After the inquest would be time enough to bother Sumptor. It was just possible, he thought, that this inquest might offer something a little different from the usual cut-and-dried routine; might bring out things or possibilities that would make an early questioning of Sumptor inadvisable.

Ten-Horse intended playing this careful. There was such a thing as being too brash. He had a hunch the Lazy D boss was dynamite.

He swept into town with a streaking cloud of dust—occasioned doubtless by the constant popping of his whip. For Jones was a man who liked a little flourish and his ten fast-stepping horses were one sure means of getting it. He never moved them leisurely—leastways not within the sight of others—but slammed them to and fro in a way that usually covered bystanders in an all-enveloping cloud of grit. And grinned when they ventured protest.

He was grinning now as he rushed his caballos corralward.

"Come a ty-yi-yippy-yippy-yo-yippy-yay! Come a ty-yi-yippy yippy-yo!" he yelled with lusty vigor.

Hoskins, the man who owned the livery stable, came running up with a face that heralded trouble. But Ten-Horse ignored him until he got the last of his remuda safely corralled. Then he stripped the saddle from Stovepipe and, hanging it upon the topmost bar, shunted him in after the rest and slammed the big gate shut.

Then he turned. "An' what are you all lathered for?" he chuckled.

"Lathered!" swore Hoskins. "You'd be lathered,

too, if yuh had t' put up with the carryin's-on I do! You don't light long enough t' git a man's-sized breath. Allus flyin' round like a pea in a bottle! Where's the blinkin' fire? Larrupin' up an' down the country like a pony express! What'n'ell yuh think this county's payin' yuh for?"

"Packin' this dod-rammed sheriff's star—that's what!" Jones told him flatly.

But Hoskins was not to be so easily propitiated. He was in no mood for joking and said so. And he said other things as well—things that popped and crackled almost loud as Ten-Horse's whip.

"Well, good grief, what's happened?" Ten-Horse asked.

"It's that slat-sided deppity you 'pointed the other day!" rasped Hoskins. "He like t've ruint Lem Ashertal—an' him with the rheumatiz so bad he can't hardly git any sleep! Come in my place las' night, that fella did, an' parked his dang ol' plug square down upon pore Lem while he was snorin'! We like t' never got 'im off! An' when we did, we practically had t' *carry* Lem upstairs. He's so dang stove up with aches an' pains he ain't been able t' do a lick o' work all day! I say we ort t' file suit ag'in that hellion!"

"Well, go ahead if it'll make you feel any better. But don't tell me; I'm only the sheriff around this place—go take it to your lawyer. Besides, I kinda like that Kasta pelican. Regular genius—writes longhand, shorthand, an' poetry! Mebbe he'll write a poem 'bout *you!*"

And, washing his hands of the matter, Ten-Horse clanked his spurs on up the street.

Spying a bit of color near the entrance to Jonathan Hardow's General Store, Ten-Horse slowed his gait a little, and his pulse began to thump. Unless he missed his guess—

He hadn't. That yonder bit of color against the sun's downsliding glare was Tony Sumptor. In person. Her own delectable self!

He blushed as he realized his eagerness.

Some vestige of that color still was evident in his cheeks as he came even with the store and saw her watching him. He cuffed his hat to a more belligerent angle, scowled at the grinning loungers, and came to a stop with his gaze admiringly fixed upon her.

"Afternoon, Tony."

"Hello, Ten-Horse."

She had a tall and willowy figure that even looked good in her present puncher's garb of cotton shirt and dust-grimed jeans. She was grace personified. She had a voice like temple chimes. Her lips were a tempting scarlet and there was a glint of copper in her hair. She was prettier, Jones thought, "than a spotted dog under a red wagon." In his eyes, bee trees were gall beside her.

There were no two ways about it; Ten-Horse Jones was bitten deep!

He came to a faltering standstill, regarding her with all the soulful gravity of a dying calf. He stopped directly in her way and without thought of the grinning loungers grouped about the porch; conscious only of her presence and the pounding of his heart.

But a thought, clicking over in his mind, aroused him like cold water. This was the girl Slow Jim had said he was going to marry! *This* was the girl he'd mentioned sending back for, once he got located and had things lined up right.

His heart cried out in protest; was there no justice in this lousy world? This girl, this vital magnetic creature, could never make a go of things with a man who packed as broad a stripe as Slow Jim Hart! Thought of Slow Jim's recently revealed shortcomings downcurled his lips with scorn.

Antonia had been moving toward him down the steps. With a sudden stiffening she stopped abruptly in her tracks. The smile went off her face and her breathing deepened sharply. With a toss of her head and flashing eyes she strode right past him, brushing him from her path as though to her his very existence were of no more import than that of the lowest worm.

He stood there stunned. Gradually it dawned upon him that she must have read the scorn and the contempt with which he'd thought of Hart, and taken it as personal; she must have thought his look of derision had been meant for her!

His soul stormed up a protest and he half turned round as though to follow. But the malice of muted sniggers recalled him to his surroundings. Looking up, he beheld a row of grinning faces. One ruffian had the guts to wink and jab an elbow at his neighbor's ribs.

Choking with chagrin and anger, Jones stormed up the street.

XII

Pony George—Creator of 'Ballards'

Inspired, no doubt, by recollection of Doris May's smile and her declared appreciation of his versifying, Pony George appeared in as fine a fettle as could properly be expected in a man who hardly twelve hours back had come within an ace of having his head blown off. Lifting his voice to the Carlsbad Caverns, he sang with lusty satisfaction.

With a choked-off curse, Ten-Horse Jones ripped something from the door, kicked the barrier open with his boot, and went tramping in with blood in his eye.

His look did not improve when he saw the sofa from Rockin'-Chair Emma's that had been pushed against the farther wall and beheld George sprawled atop it. "What's the big idea?" he roared.

George swung up to a sitting posture. "Idear?" he said with innocence. "Whadda yuh mean 'idear?' "

"Mebbe you think this is a harem?" Ten-Horse rasped.

George looked pained. "If yuh're torkin' about this sofa—"

"I *am!*"

"Wal, fer cryin' out loud! I *paid* fer it!"

"What's that got to do with it?" Arms akimbo, Ten-Horse glared. "This happens to be a sheriff's office—not a woman's rest-room! I'll thank you to keep that fact in mind. What do you think the Commissioners would say if they was t' come walkin' in an' see you luxuriatin' on that damn thing? For God's sake, act your age!"

"Now, lissen here!" George growled, getting up and wagging an irate finger underneath the sheriff's nose. "Yuh kin tork from now till doomsday an' I won't budge one blasted inch! Nossir—not on yore mortal tintype! By cripes, I jest been nearly murdered, an' I ain't hankerin' tuh repeat the experience! Not by a dang sight!"

And he stood there scowling defiantly.

"Murdered!" Ten-Horse growled. "What're you talkin' about?"

"Last night—that's what! Yuh needn't think I'm goin' tuh bed down in that blinkety-blank hotel ag'in, because I ain't! I was reachin' up t' blow the lamp, when *blam-m-m!* an' the dang thing was smashed tuh flinders! Some slat-sided, yaller-faced hole-in-the-ground took a potshot at me from that gol-rammed Striped Tiger—an' if 'is name wasn't Morris I'll eat it! Like tuh taken the side o' my haid off! Like I allus said, a chain o' dangers threads the life o' man from the diaper to the shroud—but I'll do my own applyin' fer the latter, thank yuh. An' in my own good time!"

And he reared up, throwing out his chest and glaring like a catamount. "I'm tellin' yuh flat," he declared with emphasis, "from here on out I sleep *in this office*—or I don't sleep a-tall!"

"Well," said Ten-Horse, rasping his chin, "if some fella is tryin' t' blow a window through your skull, why that puts a different complexion on the matter. I reckon you got a right to sleep here, but do it in the proper time. I don't wanta catch you sprawlin' on that sofa daytimes. An' while I think of it, you wanta put a soft pedal on that E-string beller of yours. Some of the neighbors is apt t' swear out a warrant."

But George sniffed. "Let 'em!" he said. "There ain't a man in the whole blamed county which has a decent cultivation. Jest a bunch of ignoramuses that don't know dung from wild honey! Back in Pecos we wouldn't let fellas like them outa school! They got a sayin' up there that when a Eagle Flat man kin write his own name, the Board o' Eddication gives 'im his de-ploma.

When he kin write the name of the town after it, they makes him a deppity to the marshal. But when he gits so he kin write more than that, he scratches a letter t' Sears an' Roebuck an' asts 'em t' git him a job someplace else!"

Ten-Horse scowled. "Don't crowd me too far, fella. I got a limit to my endurance." He took a bit of well-weathered wood from beneath his arm. "Is this," he said bitterly, "some of your doin'?"

"What—that sheriff sign?" George sniffed. "Hell, no!"

"You know damn well I ain't talkin' about that sheriff sign. I'm talkin' about what's on the back of that sheriff sign," Ten-Horse said, glowering ferociously. *"This!"* And he held the sign up angrily three inches from the deputy's nose.

It read:

PONY GEORGE
Creator of Ballards

When better ones is writ,
By gosh, we'll write 'em!

"You might at least," Ten-Horse told him scathingly, "learn how to spell the technical name for those atrocities you're forever turnin' out." He swore. "You can nail this sign back up—an' be damn sure you nail it with the sheriff stuff *out!* This is a sheriff's office, an' as long as the county pays the rent, it's goin' to stay a sheriff's office—*savvy?*"

"Wal," George muttered disgustedly, "can't yuh take a joke? I was on'y fixin' tuh hev some fun—"

"You better fix to get to work for a change," Ten-Horse stated soberly. "We're holdin' a inquest —or rather Doc Millbane is—tomorrow mornin' in the Striped Tiger at ten o'clock sharp. You—"

"Oh, Gawd—another inquest?" Pony George groaned. "I got my share o' them things when I was sheriffin' over to Pecos. I thought this was a peaceful country where folks raised hawses an' cattle in peace an' amity, an' loved their neighbors, an' went t' church on Sunday. An' here you go torkin' about *inquests!* They been the bane o' my existence—"

"No doubt," said Ten-Horse dryly. "You go stick on the nose-bag now while I line out some things I want you t' do between now an' ten tomorrow mornin'. Take your time an' eat a good meal. You're goin' t' need it."

Pony George rose resignedly, took his hat from a wall peg and flapped it on without enthusiasm. "Yuh wanta hear my latest verse before I go?"

"You can save that one till later," Ten-Horse grunted. "I got work to do. Go eat your supper."

"Wal, yuh don't hev tuh git tough about it. I guess I kin buy my own terbacca—"

"Here," Ten-Horse growled impatiently, and tossed over his sack. "Take that along. An' if there's any left when you get back—"

91

"Say!" George interrupted, peering curiously and squinching up his eyes. "What's that yuh got on yore shirt? No, down lower; under the arm there. You ain't never—Wal, danged ef you ain't! All over the insides of yore hands, too."

Ten-Horse pulled his gaze from his shirt and slapped it on his hands; then he clamped both brown hands on his hips and glared. "By Gawd," he blared, "I ought to comb your hair! When'd you paint that gol-rammed sign?"

George looked pained. He started a nervous backing toward the door. 'bout ten minutes before you come," he muttered faintly.

"Hell's unvarnished hinges!" Ten-Horse swore, and grabbing up George's handiwork, he let drive with a wicked fury.

But George was already out the door.

XIII

Personalities

Doc Millbane was a man who took his duty seriously. Like his liquor and his poker. Like his women. He could treat it as the occasion demanded, and appeared intent on doing so this morning. A table had been provided for him on the raised platform at the extreme north end of the Striped Tiger's main room; the platform that was customarily employed by a band hired by Morris from El Paso. This morning the band was among that crowd which had got itself wedged in here like sardines in a can. Old lazy Bill, the sagebrush fiddler, was in that expectant audience, too, and many others who had long been familiar figures in the neighborhood of Eagle Flat.

There were not many ladies present, but the male element appeared to have turned out for the occasion to a man. It would, Ten-Horse uneasily reflected, be an excellent time for the hard-working rustling fraternity to make a killing.

Doc Millbane was bustling around like an old hen with a brood of chicks; whispering mysteriously to this one, poking that one in the ribs, and generally making himself conspicuous. It was the first inquest he'd had a chance to throw since taking office, and patently he was determined to make the most of it.

George eyed him with disgust. "A all-too-common example," he confided to Ten-Horse, "o' what public office'll do to a man. Never knew a coroner yet what didn't act like the cat's pyjammers when it come tuh handlin' this kind of shiveree."

Ten-Horse nodded complacently. Taken by and large he'd found mankind to be pretty much alike the country over. All a bunch of actors, he told himself good-naturedly, ready to strut their stuff no more than you gave 'em attention.

Then he got to thinking of Tony Sumptor and craned his neck to see if she were here. He didn't locate her and turned back with a grunt at sight of Sumptor, to watch proceedings with a scowl.

Things were settling down a little now. Someone had draped a flag back of the coroner's table, and some other helpful souls had arranged a double row of chairs along one side of the platform for the jurymen. One chair had been placed at the opposite side—for the witnesses, no doubt.

Doc Millbane had brushed up his rusty clothes for the occasion, and certain rather grayish spots here and there along the front of his black coat showed where he'd endeavored with a wet rag to remove sundry adherences; very likely portions of forgotten meals.

He was impaneling his jury now, and doing it to suit himself. Very likely a number of these persons were gentlemen to whom he owed some debt or other. Sumptor, a man with influence, he had chosen arbitrarily as foreman. Then there was Hoskins, the livery stable proprietor; still talking about 'pore Lem,' and his red tongue wagging four ways from the middle. There were two bartenders on the jury; one still had his apron on. Rockin'-Chair Emma, too, had drawn a post of honor—probably for the first time in her life. Even a greaser had got on; he was owner of a low dive out on the fringe of town. Three others were tappers for the Striped Tiger. A cattle-buyer from Holbrook had one of the coveted seats. Of the two left, one went to the owner of the general store, and the other to a stranger, a plump-faced fellow with a red mustache, whose sandy hair, parted in the middle, showed slicked back like Beau Brummel's when he took off his derby hat.

Doe Millbane cleared his throat and noisily blew his nose on a large red neckerchief which he thrust sprucely into his coat's breast pocket when that ordeal was over. Then he rapped upon the table with a bung-starter.

"We are gathered here, folks, to sit upon the body of the late deceased, Mr. Charles Dunkett. It will be the duty of the jury to determine, from such facts as may be presented, whether he came by his death as the result of a felony or a justifiable homicide. By *felony,* the law means murder."

He paused to let this fact sink in.

"Now, in case it be your opinion that death resulted from a felony, it is within the jury's jurisdiction to establish—if possible—the identity of the guilty party. This court," he finished, "will now come to order. I shall clear the room if people's behavior threatens to impede the progress of this case."

He beckoned Pony George.

George dug a paper from his pocket and stood up. The crowd leaned forward expectantly. George said with due solemnity:

"The gent who gave Mister Deuces Darst an account of the killin' will kindly take the stand."

A ripple of interest spread through the Striped Tiger's crowd. But no one came forward till George growled, "You, over there in the fancy shirt. . . . No; not *you!* That fella with the egg on his chin! Yeah—*you!* Git up on the platform an' be sworn in."

The gentleman so publicly exposed wiped his chin with a furtive hand and, with his face showing bright hot color, reluctantly took the chair. The formalities were quickly disposed of and his tale was as swiftly told. A horseman dressed in black had come out of the shadows of an alley and sat glowering at Mister Dunkett in front of this saloon until Dunkett got peeved and said, 'Well, damn yuh, don't yuh like it?' The strange horseman just sat there staring. Then, finally, he had croaked in his peculiar voice, 'Dunkett, yuh rat, yo're first!' Dunkett had backed off a bit, snarling, and making as though to draw his gun—which he finally *had* drawn. He had even got in a shot before the sinister horseman moved. Then, like a flash, that hombre had thrown a knife. As Dunkett had fallen, the man had ridden off.

"Would you say," asked Coroner Millbane, "this man had attempted to disguise his voice? You spoke of the peculiarity of it, I believe."

"It was shore peculiar, all right," the witness

admitted. "But I couldn't say if he was tryin' t' disguise it. S'far as I know, I never seen the gent before or sinc't."

"Well, what did it sound like?"

"It was slow an' kinda raspy."

The Coroner put something in his mouth. "Like that?" he asked.

"No. I don't reckon so. I allow 'twas more gruff-like. Kinda harsh, if yuh get what I mean."

Doc Millbane shrugged. "I believe you told several people, including Mr. Kasta, that the man laughed as he rode off. Is that so?"

The witness nodded. "An' I shore don't wanta hear no more laffs like that! Cripes, it had me all of a shiver."

"Dunkett, you say, made the first threatening move?"

"No—no, I didn't say that. Dunkett pulled his gun first; but most any fella would've done the same, I reckon, if a guy like that was starin' at 'em the way this fella was."

"What do you mean, the way this fella was?" asked Millbane.

"Well, it was like he had it in for Dunkett plenty. He wasn't payin' no attention to the rest of us; jest starin' real mean an' ornery at Snake. Hell, didn't he say, 'Dunkett, yuh rat, yo're first?' Sure—an' he said it like he meant business, too! If you'd a seen him atop that hawse you'd sure 'a' done what snake did—only mebbe you'd 'a' done it sooner! That guy was out t' git him, an' he was goin' t' git him whether Dunkett drawed or not!"

"About that horse," Millbane said, after a look at the jury. "Couldn't any of you recognize it?"

"Well, I dunno. We was lookin' at Dunkett an' the rider. I don't 'spect any of us did much starin' at the hawse."

"Did you see if this stranger had a gun?"

"He didn't hev none; a lot of us looked for that," declared the witness positively.

"How is it that none of you tried to stop that killing?"

"Stop it?" The witness looked aghast. "Hell, d'yuh ever try t' stop a avalanche? Well, this thing was like a rock slide. Speakin' personal, I was doin' m' best t' keep outen the way. Why, that guy'd as soon 'a' bumped me off as looked at me—or anybody else. It's all right t' talk about interferin' now, but—"

"All right," said Millbane hastily. "That'll be all. You may step down, please. George, call the next witness!"

"Kinch Lee," read George from his paper.

The Bar X owner took the stand and after the formalities had been disposed of, and Lee had explained somewhat emphatically that he had not been in town on the fatal night, Ten-Horse got to his feet at a look from the coroner and said, "Mr. Lee, is it true that you've been losin' cattle lately?"

Lee growled a wrathy affirmative. "How many question are you goin' to ask me that times? I told you yesterday—"

"But this is another day," interrupted Ten-Horse suavely. "Thought mebbe you had changed your mind in the meantime. So you've been losin' cattle, have you? About how many, say, in the last month?"

"Wouldn't know," Lee answered, gruffly, though speaking slow in an evident endeavor to get his thoughts out straight. "Offhand I'd say about three hundred."

"I understand your beef cut was run off the other night."

"It was," Lee said, and swore.

"Why is it," Ten-Horse asked, "this steal hasn't been reported to my office?"

"Because I figured if I expected t' ever back my cattle get, I'd better tend that chore myself." Lee said it without compromise and there was a bit of sneer about his thin taut lips as he looked at Jones.

Ten-Horse said, "Are you intimatin' that my office ain't competent t' deal with this matter?"

"Just a minute," spoke up Coroner Millbane. "Are you sure this has got any bearing on the case in hand, Sheriff?"

"You're advisin' this jury t' pick a murderer, ain't you? Then," said Ten-Horse blithely, "my question's certainly got a bearin' on the case of

99

Dunkett's death." He settled his gunbelt more comfortably about his lean waist and looked Lee over with an evident interest. "Now, Mister Lee," he said, "let's have a answer to my question."

Lee stared about with signs of some inner disturbance, his glance—Jones noted—resting longest on the shaved-hog features of Tumbleweed Sumptor. He brought his eyes back to the sheriff with an effort, and moistened his lips several times before he spoke. "I don't see what you're gettin' at," he answered. "But since you wanta know, I'll say that I gi—I'll say I figured the odds was a heap-more likely to be in my favor if I went after them *ladrones* myself."

"Spoken like a man," beamed Ten-Horse. "Let's have the answer to this one—Didn't you help elect me to office? . . . Uh-huh; thought so. Was it your idee of a joke?"

"Certainly not!" snapped Lee. "When I office you into voted, I supposed you'd make a conscientious officer. I s'posed wrong. Hell, a fella ought t' know from at you lookin', there wasn't enough beans in your think-box t' keep you in outa the wet."

A rumble of excited mutterings broke out among the spectators. Rockin'-Chair Emma said something fiercely to the juryman beside her and Sumptor craned his neck to give her a dirty look.

"I," said Pony George above the uproar, "wouldn't take that brand of chin music off *no* man!"

Millbane rapped for order. "Let us keep personalities outta this!"

Ten-Horse grinned. "Let 'im rant if it does him good. It'd take more'n a horse-opera cow-raiser like—"

"Jest stop right there!" snarled Millbane. "This inquest'll be conducted with decorum or not at all!"

"Just as you say," murmured Ten-Horse equably, and sat down.

The crowd grew still at this unexpected development, just as Jones had hoped it would. The Coroner said, "Are you through with this witness?"

"Plumb through," nodded Ten-Horse gravely.

"Then what was the idea of gettin' this court all stirred up with—"

"I was just wonderin'," Ten-Horse observed, "about Lee's beef cut." He rose to his feet and smiled at Lee amiably. "Mr. Lee," he said, "unless you get those cattle back you won't be doin' any marketin' this year, will you?"

"I never said that," Lee denied scowling. "Certainly I'll be able to market some stuff. Those two hundred beeves aren't the total of my marketable stock by any means. I'm—"

"Mr. Lee, isn't it your customary procedure to ship from El Paso?"

Lee nodded, studying him suspiciously. "What about it?"

"Oh, nothin' much. Just another thing I been doin' some wonderin' about. I—"

"You wonder too damn much," snarled Lee, his face darkening with anger.

"Too much for my own good, you mean? Well, I shouldn't wonder. It's a family failing, Mister Lee. I take consolation, though, in realizin' how there's lots of people ain't got beans enough in the cylinder t' *do* any wonderin'. You're from Laredo, orig'nally, ain't you? Yes, well we got a sayin' up here that when a man gets so's he can write his name down at Laredo, he gits elected to the schoolboard. When he gets so's he can write Laredo after his name, he's a candidate for mayor. But when he finally learns t' spell somethin' else —if ever—he goes out t' the woodshed an' shoots himself."

The improvised courtroom had grown quieter than three mice. The coroner leaned forward puzzledly, looking from Jones to the scowling Lee and back again. The hush grew deeper as Millbane growled, "What did he wanta shoot himself for?"

" 'Cause by the time he gets smart enough t' spell ten words hand-runnin', he's old enough t' know he'll never make no money honest."

XIV

Accused of Murder!

"I object to the entire statement!" shouted a plump old gentleman of foreign mien, jumping to his feet with furious gesticulations. "I object mos' strenuously on the ground that it ees hearsay; that it ees irrelevant, incompetent, and immaterial! Furthermore, it ees a defamation of my client's character! Absolutely! It ees publique slander an' a libel!"

The hubbub in the Striped Tiger transcended all commonplaces; it took on the aspect of a session in the Senate. To be precise, the place was in an uproar and—despite Coroner Millbane's violent pounding with the bung-starter—it refused to be hushed up.

Men clapped one another on the back and chuckled. Others laughed uproariously till the tears streamed down their cheeks. "Didn't take his mouthpiece long t' git the point!" some enthusiast hooted. But there were others who glowered indignantly—among these Sumptor and the stableman. And several eyed the sheriff with distinctly malignant glances. His remark was not destined to be forgotten in a hurry. People were bandying it back and forth with rare appreciation; for, generally speaking, the Bar X owner was not popular.

Everyone was shouting, and those who shouted loudest got the most attention. Pony George's E-string bellow was right up top as he howled in the sheriff's ear:

"Brother—that was tellin' 'im!"

In his enthusiasm, the impressionable Mr. Kasta knocked off a neighbor's hat and never noticed—though the neighbor did, and swore as his forty dollar headpiece was lost beneath the surging crowd.

"Who the hell's that fossil," George demanded, "standin' there shakin' his bumbershoot? That fella that was spoutin' all that legal slop. Yeah—that ploo-to-crat with the beer-belly!"

"That," said Ten-Horse chuckling, "is the estimable Don Pedro Avalanche Jesus Maria Poder y Cuchillo—sometimes known as Cuchy, but mostly plain Pete Poder. He's the Bar X attorney. Handles all their business. Handles Sumptor's business, too. An', though you mightn't believe it, he's also lawyer for Deuces Darst. Quite a hombre."

But at last Millbane restored a semblance of order. "If we have any more demonstrations like that," he glared, "I'll clear this room an' keep it cleared!"

"He ain't man enough," George said, *sotto voce*.

Several uncouth hombres snickered, but the coroner blew his nose with dignity. He returned the red bandanna to his pocket and stared unfavorably at the attorney. "Mister Poder," he said, "I'll thank you to recall this ain't no court of law, but a coroner's court which has been called to sit upon the fate of the late lamented, Mr. Charles Dunkett. If you have any grievances, you will have to lodge them with the proper authorities."

Don Pedro Avalanche Jesus Maria Poder y Cuchillo bobbed his head with stern assurance. "I shall do so. We will sue for public defamation of character. You may count upon it. Mr. Lee is a man of influence—"

"We are not here to inquire into Mr. Lee's—"

"What I wanta know," yelped Pony George, "is *when are yuh goin' tuh 'dentify the body?*"

Color went to the tips of Millbane's ears. He said gruffly:

"Call the next witness, Mr. Kasta."

"Deuces Darst," said George, and grinned. To Jones he added without bothering to lower his voice, "Did I call the turn or didn't I?"

But Ten-Horse was intensely eyeing Darst as the gambler was being sworn in.

"I do," said Darst, and took his hand down.

"Can you identify the body?"

"Certainly. The body was that of the late Charles Dunkett."

"Did you know him well?"

"Well enough. He often took a hand in one of my games."

"I understand, Mr. Darst, that you were one of the first to examine the body." And, at the gambler's nod, "Did you see the fatal weapon?"

"Yeah," Darst said, "I saw it. A regular Arkinsaw toothpick."

"Can you think of anything else about the episode that you think might be of interest to the jury?"

"Well," Darst murmured, looking thoughtful, "I didn't see the killer, you understand, but it seems to me that it might well turn out to be the Bandit —you know, that fella down at Bloody Run."

If Darst had hauled a trench mortar into the room and pointed it at the gaping crowd, the effect would hardly have been greater than that produced by his climactic words. Rockin'-Chair Emma gasped and her eyes stuck out till a man could have hung his trousers on them. The plump-faced stranger with the red mustache leaned forward with sudden interest, and the Mexican who owned the low cantina at the edge of town hurriedly crossed himself and endeavored to shrug himself into a less conspicuous place.

"How's that?" asked Millbane nervously.

"Well, I been doin' a lot of thinkin'," Darst admitted. "Dunkett wasn't dead when I got to him. But he was pretty far gone, so when he whispered: *'Demon from hell! Demon from Hell! Gawd, Deuces—I seen Black Death a-horseback!'* why I jest nacherly figured he was out of his head. But I don't know. I been thinkin' it over an' the more I think, the more likely it seems to me that the killer was this fella at Bloody Run. I'll have more to say when you introduce the knife in evidence."

Ten-Horse elbowed George in the ribs. "You didn't tell me nothin' about Dunkett bein' alive when Deuces reached him."

"I guess not. I didn't even *know* it—nor anybody else."

The Coroner said: "Why didn't you notify the sheriff?"

"I couldn't see right off that such crazy talk would help him," Darst said smoothly. "Fact is, I can't see how it'll help him now."

"Well," said Millbane, taking a long thin package from his inside breast pocket and unwrapping it, "is this the weapon? Can you identify this knife as the one you pulled from Dunkett's body?"

The gambler took it and turned it over in his hands. "No. This is not the blade."

Millbane handed him another. "Is this?"

"Yes," said Darst at once. "This is the knife that cut Snake down. I can tell by a number of things. . . . These scratches, and this Circle Bar brand that is burned on the haft."

The crowd leaned forward tensely, everyone

striving to view the fatal knife—the blade that packed a hilt marked Circle Bar.

"Can you identify this knife as the property—"

"Do you reckon," Ten-Horse asked, "this is quite the time for that?"

Millbane flushed. "Are you tryin' to tell me how to run this inquest?"

"Not at all. But it seems to me that someone else would better—"

"Very well," snapped the coroner. "The witness may step down. Kasta, call—"

"I'd like," Ten-Horse cut in, "to recall Lee to the stand, if you've no objections."

"All right; call him," Millbane muttered in a pet.

Ten-Horse did. And when the Bar X owner had been resworn, Ten-Horse asked him casually, "Where were you on the night Charles Dunkett met his death?"

"Home," Lee answered shortly.

"All evenin'?"

"Sure—all evenin'."

"Oh, yes," said Ten-Horse blandly; "I recall now that you told me that before. Naturally, you can supply proof that will be acceptable in court?"

"This court? Certainly—"

"No," said Ten-Horse flatly; "a court of law."

Kinch Lee's florid cheeks changed color. He twisted his torso and for a moment held it rigid while his eyes swept over to Sumptor. But Sumptor's shaved-hog features revealed no expression. Lee whipped back his glance and sent it in brief scrutiny at Poder. But Poder was looking someplace else, and Lee brought his gaze back darkly.

"I don't think I'll answer that just now."

"That's all right," said Ten-Horse blithely. "I wouldn't want you to incriminate yourself for lack of good advice. Only reason I asked was on account you ownin' the Bar X—the outfit which it is alleged lost two hundred prime beeves a few nights back."

Lee stared. "Are you doubtin' that I lost 'em?"

"Did you?"

"You're did well right I damn!"

"I guess your word is good enough for most," drawled Ten-Horse easily. "That'll be all, Mr. Lee. You can step down."

But as Lee was doing so, his face not quite rid of its scowl, the lawyer jumped up with a protest. "Mr. Coroner," he cried. "I demand to know what thees man ees driving at! In w'at way could the loss of Bar X cattle be the concern of thees eenquest? We are 'ere to deescuss the facts relevant to the untimely death of Meester Dunkett—are we not?"

Doc Millbane bewilderedly nodded.

"Then for why ees the sheriff talk about cattle?"

Ten-Horse grinned, having capped them in on that one proper. "Dunkett," he said, "just before his death was talkin' about the hangin' of a certain gent. It seems to me the two things tie in nicely. Two-three nights ago Tucker Hart was lynched. I've been led to believe he was hanged for rustling—the alleged evidence resting in a brass tag, said to have come off Hart's chaps, and found on the bedground of the *stolen Bar X herd.*"

Kinch Lee stopped dead in his tracks and his cheeks went dark with rage. Sumptor's face was smooth as granite, but Poder had stepped suddenly backward as though from a leveled pistol.

The room went deathly still.

Lee snarled, "You tryin' t' hook me up with that?"

"You claim to've lost a beef cut, don't you?"

"Sure I lost it—an' it wouldn't surprise me none to learn Ol' Hart had a hand in it! We been—" And there he stopped while some of the color washed from his face. He ran a tongue across his lips. He asked less vehemently, "What's that got to do with Dunkett's death?"

"*Quien sabe?*" Ten-Horse shrugged. "Who knows? Mebbe much; or possibly nothing at all. But I been thinkin' mebbe Hart had friends. . . ."

"What," demanded Poder, "ees thees man talking about?"

"An' if he did," Jones went on as though the other had not spoken, "mebbe one of them killed Dunkett."

"I guess," Lee said with meaning, "you were close to Hart as any. Known him most of your life through pardnerin' round with Slow Jim."

"That's right; I did pardner around with Jim quite a spell. And I sure had a heap of admiration for his father. Old Hart was a pretty swell guy."

Millbane rapped on the table. "This debate has gone far enough." He scowled. "This ain't gettin' us any place. If you got any facts that are pertinent to the purpose of this gathering, Sheriff—"

"I ain't got many facts, Your Honor, but I sure got a parcel of notions," Ten-Horse murmured. "One of them notions is plenty pertinent, believe me. It's my opinion that Dunkett was one of the hombres that strung Hart up, an' that his killin' was a direct outcome of the party. An'," he added, looking Lee coldly in the eye, "if that's the case, there'll be other hombres dropped."

The forward thrust of Lee's narrow head and the flaming hate in his face promised a definite hereafter for a certain Ten-Horse Jones.

"I insist," cried Pedro Avalanche Jesus Maria Poder y Cuchillo, "that you call the nex' witness!"

"I've one more question," Jones said, holding his hand up. "Mr. Lee, where were you on the night of the twenty-third—the night these lynchers hung Tucker Hart?"

Poder waved his hands. "Don't answer! Thunder in heaven, he has no right to ask these questions! Do not answer, Señor Lee!"

"That's right. You needn't answer if you're afraid of incriminatin'—"

111

"I was home!" Lee snapped.

"Hmm. You're quite a home body," Ten-Horse smiled. "Call the next witness, George."

"Next witness is Doc Millbane."

Millbane took the oath and described the technical details of Dunkett's death, explaining that he had been killed by a knife. Then he picked up the blade with the Circle Bar burned on the handle and, mentioning that it was the fatal weapon, passed it around among the members of the jury. "I would like," he finished, "to have a reliable testimony as to the ownership of this knife."

The jury's eyes perceptibly brightened as they examined "People's Exhibit A." Sumptor put the flats of his hands to his chair and shoved himself to his feet.

Millbane regarded him expectantly. "Do you identify this knife?"

Sumptor nodded gravely. "Reckon we all know whose it is. I've seen it half a hundred times myself. I'd know it like I would my hand. It's the property of Slow Jim Hart."

Millbane nodded triumphantly and Sumptor resumed his seat.

But as the Coroner was facing front again, Rockin'-Chair Emma discontinued her gum-chewing long enough to ask, "Is that the hawg-sticker Snake was killed with?"

Millbane nodded. "That's the weapon."

When the Coroner had asked for testimony from the jury with regard to the death-blade's ownership, George had growled disgustedly into the sheriff's ear: "That one of them questions you set up las' night tuh figger?"

Now Ten-Horse got to his feet.

"I'd like to point out one little fact before everybody makes up their minds," he said. "So far as I *know,* that's the knife Dunkett was stabbed with. But we've only got Mr. Darst's word for it. The blade was not in the late deceased's body when the law took charge of it. This knife was presented by Mr. Darst who *presumably* pulled it from the corpse."

And he sat down amid a startled silence that was broken by Darst's indignant curse. "Are you insinuatin' that I switched knives?" he growled.

"Nope—only pointin' out you mighta switched 'em."

"It looks to me," Darst said, "like you're gettin' too damn brash for yore britches."

"Tut, tut," murmured Ten-Horse reproachfully. "Let's not indulge in personalities, Mister Darst. This inquest's too big a thing to consider the possibly outraged feelings of a saddle-blanket gambler. Or a cowman who's so careless as t' lose two hundred prime beeves at one crack. What we're after's *facts.*"

He appeared to ignore the black looks directed at him by Kinch Lee and the irate boss of Eagle

Flat, but scowled himself when Sumptor said, "Well, it's certainly a fact that this here blade belonged to young Jim Hart."

"An' where were *you* on the night of the twenty-third?"

"I don't remember," Sumptor said. "I guess probably I was round the ranch someplace."

"And were you around the ranch someplace when Snake Dunkett got his introduction to that knife?" Jones asked.

Sumptor smiled. "I certainly was. I was playin' seven-up with Mister Gates, the Bar X foreman."

Millbane waved his hands. "Enough of this," he grunted. "I've got other work to do. Let's get this inquest over with. Have—"

"When you goin' to sit on the killin' of Tucker Hart?" Rockin'-Chair Emma wanted to know.

"Why, uh—er—"

"That will be postponed," Ten-Horse cut in hastily, "until a few more facts are ascertained."

"Uh—yeah," grunted Millbane nervously, and mopped his face with the red bandanna. "Has the jury arrived at any verdict, yet?"

Sumptor got to his feet. "Yes," he said. "It is the unanimous verdict of this jury that Charles Dunkett met his death of a stab-wound delivered by the knife of Slow Jim Hart." He paused impressively, then added:

"It is our considered opinion that the aforesaid Slow Jim Hart be taken into custody at the earliest possible moment, and that a suitable reward for this purpose be offered by the County."

XV

Ten-Horse Talks Things Over

Having cleansed from his system by means of a man's-sized tumbler of "coffin varnish" the ugly taste left in his mouth by the coroner's inquest, Pony George made his disconsolate way back to the Sheriff's Office and dropped wearily into the chair by the desk. He had worked for some unorthodox sheriffs, but never any whose methods were so weird or better calculated to get their purveyor into Boothill in the shortest time possible, than were those of Ten-Horse Jones.

"Whew!" he muttered, mopping his face with his neckerchief, "if some of them jaspers ain't layin' pipe tuh git us run outa this locality by sundown, I'll miss *my* guess! An' that lawyer! Cripes, he was fit tuh be tied! Mebbe Jones knows what he's doin'—but it's dang sure *I* don't!"

Well, Jones hadn't returned yet, and after a few minutes of morose waiting, George decided that he might as well put in the time manufacturing further verses to his ballad of Bloody Run as to sit there doing nothing.

So he got out his pad and pencil and, wetting the latter on his tongue, screwed his dried-apple countenance into a vast array of deep-etched wrinkles and endeavored to coax the Muse.

After some while, by virtue of sundry epithets, he scrawled one full verse across the pad's top sheet. But there he stuck, and no amount of sweat appeared efficacious in untangling the snarl of his gummed-up versifier.

And so he sat for two hours musing, disdaining to look about the office to see if there were work that he could do. Then booted feet and the rattle of spur-chains advertised some gentleman's approach. The door was swung open and the gentleman stepped mincingly in.

George blinked and stared uncertainly. "Er—take a chair," he grunted.

"I'm looking for the Sheriff," announced Don Pedro Avalanche Jesus Maria Poder y Cuchillo uncompromisingly. "Where ees he?"

"Search me," said George indifferently. "I ain't his brother's keeper."

"Beg pardon?" said the caller in a most genial Spanish lisp.

"I said I don't know where he is," George shouted. He was a firm believer in the old adage that if you say a thing loud enough any foreigner will understand. "Better take a seat," he yelled, " 'cause Ten-Horse may be gone some time. He's plumb irregular in his habits."

"Irregular, señor! Thunder in Heaven, but you are too right!" Don Pedro took the proffered chair and carefully folded his hands across his bulging stomach. "It ees these so-irregular habits I 'ave come to deescuss. Of a certainty I shall wait until he gets here. Thees *hombre* shall find he has pulled the lion's beard too often—*Madre de Dios*, yes!"

Pete Poder—as Eagle Flatters were wont to call him—was a squat little man with burly shoulders. Nature had not endowed him with extra special looks; but as for cunning—Gentlemen, hush! Poder was a man who would make any com-promise that would insure an increase to his hoard of cached mazuma—an unscrupulous old devil who, it was said, had got his education by begging coppers on the streets of Mexico City in the guise of a one-legged charro.

Be that as it may, few persons in this vicinity could brag of ever besting him; and many were those who had learned to hunt a hole when Poder barked. He understood the tricks of his trade backwards and forwards—and when there were not sufficient in circulation he was not in the least averse to inventing new ones. He was one of the best hated men in West Texas.

But George was not aware of this. All *he* knew about Poder was what he had learned at the

117

inquest. His pockmarked face, though adorned with fierce mustachios, had a look of cultivation and benevolence, George thought. Undoubtedly Mr. Poder had a few beans in the box, and like enough would make an appreciative audience.

But before he could begin, a cold draft, driving abruptly across the back of George's neck, shut off his voice like a light—and just as Mr. Poder was beginning to show signs of interest.

Ten-Horse Jones stepped through the door and slammed it shut with a report that made Pete Poder jump. He did not so much as glance at George, but at Poder ominously rapped: "I heard you was lookin' for me."

"Er—it ees a mistake, señor," said Poder hastily. "I merely bring you word from the Señor Lee. *Seguro*, si that ees all."

"Oh, is that so!"

Poder swallowed. None too comfortably. There was a light in Jones' eyes he did not like. "*Please*—I am only the emissary, Señor Jones; just the go-between. Nothing personal, you onderstand. I 'ave tried to explain to Señor Lee that eet would be the height of folly—"

You sure got somethin' there!" derided Jones. "Anythin' you have to do with that hombre will be dang bad medicine—far as I'm concerned. If you wanta enjoy a long, quiet life, you better stay completely out of this. Anything Lee's got to tell me, let him come up here like a man an' say it."

Don Pedro shrugged. "But that ees just eet!" he complained. "Señor Lee has eenseest that I file suit against you. The only alternative is that you pay heem five hondred dollars cash for defamation of character an' make the public apology. Otherwi—"

"Oh, is that so!" blared Ten-Horse wildly. "Why that low-lived, 'dobe-eatin', buzzard-billed so-an'-so! You tell that swivel-eyed polecat t' sue an' be damned! You tell him if he opens his bazoo around me again, I'll come over there an' skin his hide for a saddle blanket!"

There were little sparks rousing up in Poder's eyes. But he said softly enough, "Señor Lee threatens to get your star, señor, onless—"

"Get my star! Say—when that fish-bellied short-horn gits *my* star, this country'll be drier'n jerked buff'ler with an' empty water barrel! You tell that dastard for me that if he makes another crack about me, I'm comin' over there an' feed him to the ants! Now, you get outa here an' *stay* out!"

Poder said, "But—"

"Never mind the buts!" Jones bawled. "Git out an' git out quick, lest I ferget myself an' do you a mortal injury! Git, gol-darn you—*git!*"

George wiped a perspiring forehead. "Wal, yuh've done it now, I reckon. First yuh rile Darst, an' Lee, an' that cold-jawed Sumptor hombre. Now yuh go an' pick on this black-leg lawyer fella. Ef we ain't both poisoned in our sleep, it'll be a miracle of Divine Providence!"

"Miracle, hell!" growled Jones. " 'F those bozos try any rough stuff aroun' me, I'll pistol-whip 'em clear across hell's furnace! I'm gettin' fed up with the politics of this country! It's time we had a new deal!"

"Wal, mebbeso," George said. "But it seems like if you was jest loadin' it onto Lee at that inquest so's tuh git attention away from Slow Jim's knife, yuh was shore pilin' up one mighty tough dividend fer yo'self. That Lee pelican will be out tuh git yore scalp!"

Ten-Horse snorted. "Any time that guy can put the skids under me will sure be one decrepit day! I was out t' make 'em mad, all right; an' I reckon I done it—"

"Brother, yuh shorely did!"

"Yeah, well, I had a dang good reason, too. It strikes me, George, that Darst an' Lee an' this greaser lawyer are all hooked up together. I can't quite figure Sumptor, though. He *ought* t' be in with them others, but it looks uncommonly like he's settin' pat. Here's the lay:

"Sumptor's been needin' Hart's water. Hart wouldn't give 'em a drop. In his defense we can say that if he had, Sumptor woulda fed him off the range—"

"Yuh mean Sumptor would have quartered his cattle on Hart?"

120

"Like a flash! Never was no love lost between them two. Well, Hart knew what would happen the minute Sumptor's cattle got a taste of his water. So he fenced it in good an' solid, an' him an' Slow Jim hung around with rifles. Towards the last I reckon they dropped a few of Sumptor's bulls. Anyways, Sumptor's punchers come over one mornin' with Bill McCash an' drove the Lazy D stuff clean off Hart's range—takin' off, I shouldn't wonder, some of Hart's cattle in the bargain.

"Then one evenin' Hart gits hung. The story's spread how Hart is the chief of these rustlers that's been workin' this country over. But I don't believe it for one holy minute. Hart was a square-shooter. He mighta shoved a few nesters out in his time, but he never snaggled his rope on another man's cows. Yuh can stick a pin in that!"

"Anyhow, the rumor got round that Hart was headin' these rustlers. Then comes the story of the Bar X beef cut sproutin' wings an' of one of Hart's chaps ornaments bein' found on the bedground of the rustled cut. If you're askin' *me,* it's too dang pat fer truth!"

"It does sound awful good," George admitted seriously. "What yuh reckon happened?"

"I don't think the cut was stole at all. I think the whole thing was a frame-up t' get Hart out of the way so's Sumptor an' Lee could get that water!"

"That why yuh pestered Lee s' much about his beef cut?"

121

"Partly, yeah. But I had another reason. George," Ten-Horse looked at his deputy intently; "I was talkin' with a fella last night which had just come up from the south a piece. He claimed he seen a whole bunch of Bar X stuff jest south a bit from the Van Horn Mountains—"

"Ha!" exclaimed George excitedly. "I guess that proves the cut was stole, all right!" He smacked his thigh. "They're headin' that beef fer—"

"Yeah?" Ten-Horse looked at him pityingly. "You guess wrong, then. This fella seen three four hands with them critters—an' Gates was bossin' the hands."

"Gates!" George's jaw sagged and his eyes bugged out. "Gates—yuh mean Kinch Lee's *foreman?* Wal, the dirty, low-down hound!"

"Don't be a sap!" Ten-Horse grunted. "Gates wasn't stealin' them steers. He was obeyin' orders."

George's eyes came open wider, bright and blue. "Yuh mean tuh say Kinch Lee was fixin' tuh rustle his own cattle? Wal, I'll be a knock-kneed gopher! Fixin' tuh steal his own beef! That's shore comin' it pretty low!"

"It is," Ten-Horse agreed. "But like I said, Lee an' Sumptor was out t' get Hart's water. 'Course, Sumptor—if he's mixed up in this—may not know Lee's pulled a fake steal. Lee may be runnin' in a fast one on 'im. But what I'd like t' know is jest what's the connection between

Sumptor an' Lee? Sumptor needs that water a dang sight worse'n Lee does. Why should he ring Lee in on it when he could have framed Hart by himself?"

"Mebbe he didn't hev nothin' tuh do with Hart's hangin'," George suggested. "Or, if he did, mebbe he figgered 'twould look too raw was he t' claim Hart had rustled *his* steers. He wouldn't want tuh git mixed up in no hangin' bee—not public, anyhow."

"No, I guess not. Still, there's somethin' there that ain't showin' on the surface. I won't be satisfied," Ten-Horse said, "till I get to the bottom of this business."

"What about that 'further testifyin' ' Darst was gonna do when the knife was introduced?" George wondered.

Ten-Horse grinned. "I reckon he got cold feet when I started askin' questions. He didn't like it a heap when I suggested he mighta switched them knives—an' he mighta done so, at that! I wouldn't put it past him. Well, you better go put on the nose-bag, now. I'm gettin' hungry myself. You go ahead, an' don't set makin' calf's eyes at that black-haired biscuit-shooter all night, either. We got plenty t' keep us busy now."

"That biscuit-shooter ain't no concern o' mine," George told him loftily. "I ain't the marryin' kind."

XVI

The Sheriff Fights His Hat

Ten-Horse Jones was roused from thoughts of Sumptor's daughter by the sharp flat crack of a rifle.

He was on his feet in an instant. Three swift paces took him through the door. He stopped in the twilight's curdled shadows, bent a little forward from the waist and with both brown hands resting on his guns.

The quietness of death had fallen across this town's traditional noises, and across the drifting shadows came plainly the melancholy baying of a distant hound.

For tight grim moments after the last faint echoes of the shot had dimmed, Jones stood there, to one side of the bar of light spilled outward by the open office door.

Night wind cascading from the slopes of Tabernacle Mountain whipped up a trail of dust along the street and fluttered the purple scarf at Ten-Horse's throat.

And still he did not move, but stood there silent, strained, and peering; each hand clamped about the smooth, worn butt of a holstered .45.

What had happened? Who had fired that shot,

and why? Had it found its mark, or gone winging off across the sandy waste? Was it some exuberant cowboy letting off his steam?

Jones thought not; the town was too still. More likely it was ambush lead, loosed with swift unsighted stealth and deadly intent. Or—was this some kind of trap being cunningly baited by his enemies?

Ten-Horse tensed, straining slowly forward, striving to cleave the gloom with narrowed eyes. A sudden thought flipped over in his mind. Was this another lyncher killing—a follow-up of the incident of Dunkett's death?

And then he caught the clump of hurrying bootsteps as there came a lull in the wind's definite sound. Some man was lunging toward him through the flowing curtain of these shadows.

There—yes! He caught the blurred outline of a moving figure; a lurching runner whose heavy breath was labored.

The sheriff straightened alertly, his grim eyes keened to catch the taint of trickery, one gun leveled and free of leather. "Halt!" he called out softly, and lined his pistol straight upon the target. "This is the Law a'talkin' at you, fella."

There was no reply—nor any slackening of the on-coming runner's pace. Jones could hear the fellow's breathing now like the pant of a heated hound. Then suddenly a voice ripped through the shadows:

"Hurry! Fer cripes sake, Ten-Hawse—git back inside an' douse thet light!"

Jones whirled inside the office; blew the lamp with a single breath. A clatter of boots on the steps outside, and Pony George slid in and slammed the door.

"Gawd!" he gasped. "They dang nigh got me that time! *Whew!*"

Jones crouched beside the window, peering out; his pistol ready. But he caught no sign of other figures in the deepening murk outside.

He growled irritably: "What the devil's up? Was that you doin' that shootin'?"

"Who—*me?*" George cried, and snorted. "I sh'd say not! All I was doin' was runnin'! Can yuh see anythin' out there?"

"No," Jones growled, and holstering his gun, he lit the lamp.

George was a wild-eyed figure. His clothes were dusty and his eyes had a too-bright gleam. He still was breathing heavily and his face was like a hunk of chalk.

"Pull yourself together," Ten-Horse muttered. "Don't stand there like you seen a ghost."

"Ghost! I dang near *was* one!" complained George indignantly. "By cripes, that Morris polecat'll git me yet, ef I ain't careful!"

"You got Morris on the brain," jeered Ten-Horse. "He prob'ly wasn't within a block of you—"

"Wal, that's what *you* think. Listen—I'd left the

hash-house an' was jest abreast that alley what runs between the Striped Tiger an' the gen'ral store, when WHAM-M-M! that guy lets go an' like tuh took the top o' my haid off! An' if yuh think I'm crazy, take a look at this yere hat!"

Sure enough. Lead had been through George's hat and left its mark.

"If you think it's Morris," Ten-Horse said, "why don't you swear out a peace-bond? Make him put up three–four hundred dollars an'—"

"No, thanks!" George said grimly. "I got too much consideration fer my hide. I—"

He broke off as the door swung open and Ten-Horse shifted in his chair.

"Howdy. Hope I ain't crashing any conference, gents."

"Nope." Ten-Horse Jones' shrewd eyes surveyed inscrutably the man standing paused by the door. "C'mon in, Darst, an' make yourself to home. We don't stand on ceremony here—as I guess you've noticed." He grinned wryly. "What's on your mind this evenin'? Get roused out by that shot?"

"Shot? No, I didn't hear any," Darst said easily. "I come over to tell you young Hart's in town again. Better move sharp if you're aiming to get your hands on him."

A voice from over Darst's shoulder gruffed: "Don't work up no lather, folks. 'F you'll move aside, Darst, I'll come in."

Darst moved as though a pistol prodded him,

and put his back against a wall, his eyes going over Slow Jim from head to toes, and without releasing a glimmer of his thoughts.

Slow Jim came in and shut the door.

"You may not know it, hombre," Ten-Horse told him, "but you've pulled a dang bad mistake in stickin' your head in here. We had an inquest on Dunkett this mornin'—"

"An' the coroner's jury," Darst cut in smoothly, "decided that Snake was killed by a stab-wound inflicted by your Bowie. They recommended you be taken into custody at the earliest possible minute, an' that a suitable reward be tacked up by the County for the purpose."

"Unfortunately," Ten-Horse added, not without malice, "no reward has been put up yet, so no one's apt to bend a gun on you just yet." And he looked at Darst significantly.

Darst's pale face revealed no more emotion than the edges of the deck of cards protruding from his waistcoat pocket.

But young Jim Hart's open countenance betrayed amazement, chagrin, and finally a fleeting glimpse of downright horror. *"My knife?"* he whispered. And shuddered when Ten-Horse nodded.

"But it couldn't—"

"It was," said Darst's cold voice. "I pulled it from Dunkett's chest right after he died."

"Oh!" A light as of understanding suddenly broke across Slow Jim's face. "I see now what you meant when you told me you'd got the note—"

"Note! What note is that?" demanded Ten-Horse brusquely.

There was a keener, tauter look to the gambler's guarded features. He folded his arms across his chest and stared at Hart, his veiled eyes holding some message meant for Hart alone.

But Slow Jim was not heeding him. He was looking at his one-time pardner, and the frown between his eyes showed the swiftness of his thought. "The note," he said, "that Deuces found wrapped about the haft of the knife he pulled from Dunkett."

"Oh! So there was a note, was there!" Ten-Horse growled, and flung his look at Darst. "Pity you didn't mention that note at the inquest, *Mister* Darst!"

"I was goin' to," remarked the gambler coolly. "But you didn't give me any chance. If you'll think back, you'll recall I told Millbane that I'd have somethin' more to say when the knife was introduced into the evidence."

"It's nice you got that alibi handy," Jones said through his teeth. "Daggone nice an' *lucky!* Gettin' info'mation outa you's like tryin' t' scratch yo' ear with yo' elbow! But you can speak your piece right now—what was in the note?—*Wait!*" He held his hand up, saying to Hart across his shoulder: "Did you see this precious note, Jim?"

"No."

129

"All right, Darst; let's have it."

"It said," Darst murmured, " 'The least shall be first. Let the greater culprits take heed an' ponder the ways of Fate. Death rides the range.' It was signed by a miniature black horseman."

"You mean one of them damn horse sketches?" demanded Ten-Horse incredulously.

Darst nodded, the corners of his lips curling faintly. "The trademark of the Bandit—the fella from Bloody Run."

But Jones had himself in hand again. "Your memory's sure a daisy," he commented cynically. "Where's the note?—I wanta see it."

"Sorry—I tore it up."

"You tore it up!" blared Ten-Horse. "Why, you gol-rammed fool! Didn't you know that thing was legal evidence?"

"I'm afraid I wasn't thinkin' about evidence at the moment." The gambler shrugged. "However, I've given you the message verbatim."

"Ver—*Hell!*" Jones snapped, and cursed with a wicked passion.

"Guess I'll be siftin' along," Slow Jim said, and began a cautious backing toward the door.

Darst looked at Ten-Horse significantly. Ten-Horse returned the stare with interest and kept on swearing.

The gambler's eyes went narrow and he wheeled his head toward young Jim Hart. "You better wait," he purred, and dropped his shoulders forward with both hands flexed at his sides.

But Slow Jim wasn't waiting, and something in his look said that it was not the time for monkey-shines. He reached the door and thrust his left hand out behind him, feeling for the knob. His gaze clung raggedly to Darst and his mouth was clamped in a white grim line.

The door came open. Then things happened with a terrifying suddenness.

One moment he was crouched before them ominously—an animal at bay. The following instant, hand dropping to his gun, he whirled and leapt headlong through the open doorway.

Flame bit its crimson streak through the black of night as a shot smashed jarring echoes. The office lamp, bracketed to the wall above the sheriff's desk, snuffed out in a tinkle of shattered glass.

A palpitant hush descended with the resulting murk. A low, rasping whisper floated through the room. Its sound was no louder than a bat's wings covered with spider's web.

"Kinch Lee will be the next snake wrigglin' down the Boot Hill trail. Then I'm droppin' Darst. Then that lyin' two-faced Tumbleweed—"

The rest was lost in the clatter of rushing hoofs as a horse fled wildly through the night.

Snapping a match to flame, Ten-Horse Jones crossed the creaking floor to a cupboard from which he presently dug an unbroken mantle for the lamp. It was astounding what a difference a little lamplight made. The place looked actually cheery!

"Well, that's that," he said, and whistled softly.

"It sure is, brother!" George concurred. "An' fer one, I don't want no more of it—that dang shootin' liked t' jarred my liver loose! Cripes, what a country! Why any gent would wanta be a deppity fer, is shore beyond Yours Truly!"

Crossing the room, Ten-Horse closed the door and bolted it. "We had company enough for one night, anyhow. Fetch out that bottle from the bottom drawer. It's sure a helluva life, as the dog told the flea before he bit it. When did Darst clear out?"

"Don't ast *me!* I got all I kin do keepin' skin an' bones together without tryin' tuh keep cases on *that* bird! I thought yuh said he was boss of this here burg?"

"He *was,*" Jones muttered drily. "But it looks a heap like King Colt's applied fer the job of city manager—an' standin' a dang good chance of gettin' it. What do you think of Darst holdin' out on that note?"

"I cain't think," George grumbled. "My dang ears is ringin' too durn much! How do yuh know there *was* a note?"

"Didn't Jim say so?"

"Sure—but he didn't see it! I don't like this business none whatever *a*-tall! Fer two cents I'd unpin this star an' pull m' pin fer fresher pastures. A risin' poet has got no business monkeyin' with hangin' bees an' shoot-outs!"

"Aw—dry up an' leave me think," snarled Ten-Horse. "It's too dang bad about you! How'd you like t' be standin' in *my* boots now? Here I been figurin' to do a little sparkin' with Tony Sumptor, an' now the guy what says he's goin' t' marry 'er pops up again—an' him my ol' sidekick, at that! You ain't even got on shoutin' terms with hard luck yet, an'—*Say!* leave anyways one-half a swaller of that stuff for *me!*"

"Sorry—it's too late now. You shoulda spoke sooner," George said, and tossed the empty bottle out the window. "Y'orta git that winder fixed. Don't yuh know it's comin' on winter?"

Ten-Horse swore. "By Gee, I ought to unpin that star *for* you!"

But George just sniffed. "Don't trouble yoreself. I'm feelin' better now. That was good stuff, Jones. Yuh ort tuh git some more of it."

"You got a gall like a Japanese monkey!" Ten-Horse grunted bitterly. "The las' damn bottle I had, too!"

"Wal, live an' learn," George commiserated. "Looks like yuh'll hev tuh go after Slow Jim now, an' no mistake. After that shootin' an' the way Darst'll be a-tellin' it, I don't see's there's anythin' we kin do but git out a reward that dawggone jury ordered."

Ten-Horse looked at him. "Do you think Jim stabbed Snake Dunkett?"

"Lord, I dunno. You know 'im better'n I do."

"I knew the old Jim; but I don't know this new one at all," Ten-Horse growled. "He's got me fightin' my hat."

"Funny the way some fellas can change. I recall . . ."

But Ten-Horse wasn't listening. "After all," he muttered, "it sure don't seem like a guy what would pull his freight no more'n somebody swung his ol' man, would hardly have nerve enough t' go jabbin' a knife in a gun fighter."

"Sure don't—but he ain't *pulled* his freight, yet," George pointed out.

Ten-Horse grunted. Then, bending abruptly forward, he picked up a bit of paper from the floor nearby the door. "What's this?" He smoothed it out and frowned, "Say—take a look at this, George."

George read:

"Pull out of this now before you git hurt."

There was a miniature sketch of a silhouetted horseman below the words.

"The Bandit!" George gasped, startled. Then, as the implications of that note struck home, he licked his lips and sent a furtive glance about. "Yuh—yuh don't suppose he's jokin', do yuh?"

"Hardly! What I want to know is how'n hell did he get that note inside here?" Ten-Horse looked at the deputy thoughtfully. He seemed about to make a pertinent observation. But something must have changed his mind. For he closed his mouth up tightly and began a nervous pacing back and forth.

Approximately ten minutes after the foregoing conversation took place, a masked and dark-clothed rider stepped from the clustered shadows at the side of the Sheriff's Office and moved away on soundless feet. At a point some twenty paces up the street he stepped to a hitchrail, ducked beneath it, and rose to the saddle of a sleek black gelding. There he sat a moment, looking back. Then he kneed his black beast forward, swinging slanchways toward the left where he vanished in the deeper murk.

XVII

The Man in the Derby Hat

"Wal," growled George, "we gonna issue that reward or not?"

Ten-Horse swore beneath his breath. "Somebody oughta corral that swivel-eyed jury an' boil 'em in lard! Danged if they ain't made me more trouble in a han'ful of minutes than I'm apt t' unravel in the rest of my life. Mind you, I ain't sayin' Jim never wound up Dunkett—'cause he might of. But I don't believe it! An' I ain't got no overpowerin' cravin' to go take that job to the printer, neither. When a guy has been your pardner, sharin' your blankets, ridin' with you, raisin' the same hell you raise an' clawin' with you outa the same tight places—I say it's a mighty meechin' thing t' go an' raise your hand again' him!"

"Yeah," George nodded; "it kinda puts yuh on a spot."

He studied the sheriff covertly, chewed the scrawny ends of his mustache, and finally murmured, "But yuh gotta look out fer Number One in *this* world, dang it! 'F yuh don't, nobody else is gonna dig in fer yuh. An' 'f yuh don't git that notice posted pronto, them County Comm's is a heap li'ble tuh lift yuh outen office— special' if that tinhorn gambler goes yawpin' round 'bout how yuh had Jim right here in the office an' let 'im git away! They ain't goin' tuh like that, Ten-Hawse."

"Are you tellin' me?" Ten-Horse sighed. "An' the hell of it is, Jim looks to be guiltier'n hell! But, dang it, that boy used t' be my pardner, George!"

"Sure—sure, I know," George muttered hastily. "But it's either git up that reward or git throwed out, as I see it. You ain't got much choice."

"But soon's you sick the law on a fella," Ten-Horse grunted gloomily, "there ain't but two courses lift 'im—give up an' hope for the best, or

136

go on the dodge an' end up by goin' hog wild."

Ten-Horse stared morosely at the ceiling. "I reckon, accordin' to rights, I'd oughta go peltin' after Jim right now—on account of that shootin'. Shucks; let's just call that a kinda last chance, George. 'Course, we're goin' to have to post that notice 'fore long. But we'll let it slide a bit an' see how things shape up. 'F Jim goes on the rampage again we'll just nacherly have t' pull him in. Friendship can only go so far."

George nodded. "Yo're right—dooty is dooty. Uh, by the way, Ten-Hawse—yuh got any more of that good smokin' yuh loaned me the other day?"

Ten-Horse scowled. "You ain't paid *that* back yet."

"But I will," George promised, "jest as soon as I git paid. Why, back in Pecos the mothers are allus pointin' me out to their kids. They say, 'Lookit that fella, sonny—look 'im over well. His word's worth more than Gov'ment bonds! Ef you grow up t' be haff as reliable as—' "

"All right," grunted Ten-Horse, cutting it short. "Better leave somethin' for the preacher t' say after you're dead an' gone. Take this cigar that black-haired biscuit-shooter slipped me, an' don't say I ain't no sport."

For long moments after the sheriff had left the office, Pony George stood there goggling and with his mouth wide open. Then he swore. Looking at the cigar he was holding in his hand, he swore again, indignantly. He dashed the offending weed to the floor and stamped upon it in a rage.

"Dad-blast 'im!" he muttered vehemently. "He kin git me madder'n any gent I ever knowed! 'Take this cigar that black-haired biscuit-shooter slipped me!' " he mimicked. "The slat-sided, yeller-faced babboon! I ort tuh ram it down his throat!"

The six o'clock stage from El Paso had not arrived the following morning by eight-fifteen. At nine, George, coming to the door of the Sheriff's Office at the sound of hurried hoofs, saw a hatless rider heading a dust cloud into town. Down the street he tore at a headlong gait, to pull his mount to a slithering stop that flung grit and pebbles against the swearing George.

"What the hell ails yuh?" George demanded, cuffing himself off. "Fella'd think yuh was the Pony Express or—"

"Hobble yo' jaw," the rider snapped, scowling. "Where's the Sheriff?"

"Still poundin' his ear—if yuh're askin' *me*. What's up?"

"Hell's Crick! The stage went off the cliff up in them mountains no'thwest of Lasca round five o'clock this mawnin'! Some'un had piled a bunch of boulders on the road this side of that hairpin bend an'—"

"Damnation!" George swore. "Now who coulda done it?" He peered at the news-bringer owlishly. "Was anybody hurt?"

"Wa'n't nobody aboard, I reckon, 'cept Janicklo, the driver. He wa'n't hurt much—musta broke his neck soon's they landed in the gulch. I got there a leetle after five-fifty-eight. Somebody'd been through Janicklo's pockets, an' the mail sack's gone. You better root the Sheriff out—I'll lay you ten t' one this is some more o' the Bandit's work."

"That fella's a desp'rit character," George muttered, shaking his head.

"Desp'rit!" echoed the messenger with a hard look, "that fella's slick as a gun barrel! An' you wanta watch yore step if you're goin' after him. He wouldn't think no more of puttin' a winder through yore skull than he would of wringin' a chicken's neck."

George swallowed uncomfortably. "I don't allow I'll be goin' after him," he said wishfully; "somebody's got tuh hold this office down—'cordin' tuh the Sheriff." He eyed the messenger confidentially. "Now I personally," he informed him, "woulda had this dang robber in the hoosegow by this time—in the hoosegow or stretched out on the prairie, one. Ten-Hawse beats aroun' the bush too much. He's allus gatherin' up a posse an' gallivantin' round like hell emigratin' on cartwheels! Too many men; too much noise; a heap too many hawses. Cripes—

that vingaroone would know they was comin' 'fore they got within forty miles! The way t' ketch this Bandit is tuh go out after him solo."

"Well, you might be right at that," admitted the messenger, impressed. "Jones is too dang easy-goin' to amount t' much as sheriff. I said that before he was elected, an' I'll say it ag'in. A swell guy, but—"

"Yeah," George conceded; "one o' Gawd's noblemen. Ef he had my experience he'd be a world-beater—no doubt about it. Nacherly, though, I ain't goin' tuh antagonize him by offerin' suggestions. He's kinda touchy that way. Wal," he sighed, "I expect I better git him up."

He slammed the office door, untied his caricature of a horse from the tangle of knots that anchored the decrepit steed to the hitch rack, and stepped cautiously into the saddle. "You better come along with me," he told the messenger. "Ten-Hawse may wanta question yuh. Might even want yuh to j'ine the posse. Giddap, there, Dynamite."

When the fall sun stood directly overhead, George clumped his frazzled boots to the Alamo Restaurant, stepped inside, and took a stool at the counter. Doris May came bustling from the kitchen. She set some other customer's grub down absent-mindedly and came at once to where George sat, giving him a radiant smile. "Good

morning, Sheriff," she said with friendly direct-
ness. "So the Bandit's up to his old tricks again,
is he? It's a wonder the stage people don't put
on a shotgun messenger."

"I expect they ain't got enough," George
answered. "Or too dang tight, most prob'ly."

"Say—" Doris May said, lowering her voice,
"we got some of the finest prairie oysters today
that ever came off a ship. You better book yourself a order quick, 'cause they're goin' faster than
snow in June."

"Don't care ef I do," George grunted. "An' let
me hev some more o' that swell cawffee, too. An'
a stack o' wheat, plate of rolled oats, a sizzlin'
steak, some collyflower, beans, an' shamrock
cobblers. An'—yeah, let me hev a side dish o'
bacon an' eggs. An' a slab o' custard pie fer
dessert. I don't know what ails my appetite, lately.
Been fallin' off somethin' awful. Got me worryin'
like a bullfrog lookin' fer rain in Arizona."

"Mebbe I better serve this order in courses,"
Doris May suggested.

"Wal," said George dubiously. "If you think it's
best. I got a heap o' faith in yore good jedgment.
Never see a woman with haff yore sense—"

"Why, Mister Kasta!" Doris May said, and
blushed with pleasure.

After the bulk of noonday customers had
bolted their food and departed, George sat on, still
going strong. Doris May came from the kitchen

wiping her hands on her apron. She stopped across the counter from him and lounged there hipshot and smiling.

"It does me good to see you eat so hearty."

"Hearty—hell, my appetite's all shot tuh splatters," grumbled George. "I ain't ate a decent meal since some dang gopher—which I think is Morris—took a shot at me! An' that dang bozo what put a slug through m' hat last night sure didn't improve the sitsiashun none! I tell yuh, Doris May, I sure wouldn't recommend this burg tuh no gent suff'rin' with nerves!"

Doris May's fine eyes showed a real alarm. "Do, for goodness sakes, be careful, George. I surely wish I hadn't ever persuaded you to take a job as Ten-Horse's deputy. What does the Sheriff think?"

George shook his head. "Don't ask me! He's a close-mouthed gopher if I ever saw one! An' say—how come yuh t' give him that cigar las' night?"

"Cigar?" Doris May looked puzzled. "I didn't give him any cigar. Whatever gave you that impression?"

George's jaw was sagging open. He closed it with a smothered oath. "Yuh didn't, eh? Humm!" He nodded grimly. "If yore father's round I'd like a word with him."

"My father—Why, Dad's been dead goin' on fourteen years. I haven't any kinfolks living—"

"Wal, that whoppy-jawed liar!" George exclaimed. He said—"

"Has that fool Ten-Horse been loading you, George?"

"I'll load *him!*" George cried. "That damn guy's got more durn brass than a military band!"

"Don't pay any attention to him," she explained. "Ten-Horse Jones is known as the greatest kidder in thirteen states. Why, I wouldn't even put it past him to have fired those shots—"

George was scowling. "Nope," he growled. "He never did that shootin'—first time he wa'n't in town, an' las' night he was at the office when I got there."

"Take it easy, now," she murmured. "But there's a man in a derby hat at a table near the door that seems to know you. He's been watching—"

"Huh? *Who*—where?" George growled, and swung round upon his stool suspiciously. His mouth dropped abruptly open. He snapped it shut with a click of teeth. He'd spotted the fellow instantly and the sight did nothing to heighten his sense of well-being.

It was the derby-hatted juryman that Doris May had indicated.

He was a plump-faced, chunky fellow with sandy hair and a red mustache. He was clad in blue serge store clothes and had his feet tucked into box-toed yellow shoes. The suit, though neatly pressed, showed definite luster in several places, and a suggestive bulge beneath the left armpit.

George was impressed. He was more so when the man, as though sensing his scrutiny, looked up and George beheld his face. It was plump and genial. At one time or another in the past the nose had apparently been broken and had been reset —if at all—with haste and little judgment.

But these things, though interesting in themselves, were not what held George rigid. The fellow had the greenest pair of eyes he'd ever looked into—hard and cold as jade. They seemed to be regarding George with a close and gathered interest.

George gulped and turned around; in his haste upsetting the newly-poured cup of coffee Doris May had set at his elbow.

"Oh! Did you burn yourself?" she gasped, fluttering about him with a napkin, and leaning across the counter in a way that made him blush. "I'm *so* sorry, George. It was—"

"Aw, that's all right," George muttered, getting to his feet. "I gotta be hurryin' down the street. I uh—er, jest recollected a engagement I dang near forgot. Charge that meal to the County, Doris—"

"But George, I can't do that. The boss would—"

"Okey," George said, frowning. "Put it on the cuff till payday. I can't stop tuh argue now—that fella mightn't wait. I'll be seein' yuh later, Doris."

And he cat-footed it for the door.

But just as he was stepping through it, a look cast across his shoulder disclosed the hard green eyes of the derby-hatted man still upon him. He read in them a light of interested speculation that appeared to bode no good to Ol' Man Kasta's little son George.

"Gee-*rusalum!*" he muttered, clambering into his saddle. "Ef that guy ain't a dick, may I be hanged fer a whoppy-jawed Chinaman! Now what does *he* want aroun' here?"

XVIII

"Me an' Ten-Hawse Jones!"

It was after nine that night when the Sheriff's disgruntled posse rode wearily into town after their long and uneventful search for the elusive robber who had become notoriously known as "The Bandit of Bloody Run."

"*No,* we didn't ketch him!" one of the possemen told George. "We never even follered 'is blame tracks more' n haff a hour," he added disgustedly. "Not even a 'Pache Injun coulda follered 'em more than two whoops an' a holler! That dang scorpion is cuter than a bug's ear. Smart—by cripes, you wouldn't hardly believe it, but that durn hellion was a-watchin' us all the time! Ev'ry

145

three–four hours we'd find a note stuck up on a stick with some dang smart-alec remark writ on it!" He shook a significant finger under George's nose. "That hombre's plumb cultus—an' smarter. than a whip!"

"Yeah—we'll make 'im smart when we git a-holt of him," George growled. "He can only last so long. An' if he ever gits Ten-Hawse's mad up, we'll rope 'im quicker'n hell could scorch a feather! They ain't no use grumblin'. You mark my words, Mister; that fella's about reached the end of his rope!"

"Don't talk foolish," the posseman snapped. "Ten-Hawse'll never git that boy—why, Ten-Hawse couldn't even find a purple camel in a snowdrift! That fella run circles all around us an' we never even spotted him onct!"

And the irate citizen stamped off in sullen resentment.

George shook his head and went plodding back to the office. "It's too dang bad Ten-Hawse ain't got my brains," he muttered. "Such a dang fine cuss, too—it's a shame. But I reckon that jasper was right. Ten-Hawse jest wa'n't cut out tuh be no hero. He's got the looks . . . but he jest don't hev no savvy. Takes brains tuh ketch these ring-tailed rannyhans like that Bandit. Now I could do it, I reckon; but—shucks I never could look poor Ten-Hawse in the eye again. It's too bad he ain't got the git-up-an'-go Colt Anders had. Now there was

146

a *man!* He never let nothin' git him down—not even when they took his star away an' stuck a price on his head to boot! Colt jest waded right in an' showed them blame know-it-alls he had more sense in his little finger'n all the rest of 'em put t'gether!"

Back at the office, George turned up the lamp a bit and, pulling his pad and pencil from a hip pocket, settled himself comfortably in the sheriff's chair and prepared to woo the Muse. Sure needed wooing, too, he mused reflectively. He hadn't written a line since the night that unknown gent had thrown a slug through his hat.

Then suddenly he paused, stiffening. Someone was coming down the walk outside. Ever since the last time he'd been shot at, George had been a mite nervous. "Edgy" was the way he put it.

He glanced at the clock. 9:48 p.m.

He was lowering a hand toward his holster when the door came open and a man slipped in, closing it softly behind him and standing with his back against it.

George sat petrified!

Completely in black was the man before him clad. Black boots, black chaps, black shirt and vest and neckerchief. A black hat was pulled well down above his eyes, and a black scarf was pulled well up across the bridge of his nose. There was a big gun staring ominously from his hand and his eyes were glowing like two hot coals.

"The Bandit!" George gasped, and sat there staring, speechless.

"Yeah—the Bandit," the black-clad man mocked grimly. "I hear you been writin' a poem about me. Where is it, *hombre*—talk quick. An' don't make no crazy moves, 'cause my trigger-finger's mighty itchy!"

George gulped—and gulped again.

"Uh—er, Great Guns, pardner—I ain't writ no poem about *you!*" he quavered. "I jest sorta borried yore name fer the title of my ballad. I—"

"Yeah. You ain't the only one that's borried it— but yo're like t' be the last! Fetch it up, now! Where is it?"

"I—I ain't got it with me," George muttered, having trouble with his Adam's apple. "Not—not all of it, that is. There's ten verses—the las' ten," he added uncomfortably, "on this here pad, but—"

"Well, what you waitin' for? Hand 'em over!" the Bandit rasped.

George bent down, preparatory to sliding the pad across the floor. But the Bandit growled: "No yuh don't—I'm up to all them tricks. Bring it over here. *An' bring it quick!*"

George made haste to obey—such haste, in fact, that he tripped on his spurs and went down flat upon the floor.

"None o' that now!" growled the masked hombre, flourishing his gun. "Get up on yore hind feet an' hand me that pad!"

George rose from the dust as pale as ashes and with a trembling hand extended his verses; believing that they might, indeed, be his ten very last.

The Bandit took one look at them and tossed the pad aside. "*That* stuff!" he sneered contemptuously. "Do you hev the guts t' call that *poetry?*"

A tide of red washed the pallor from George's cheeks. "By cripes," he muttered resentfully, "if yuh kin do better yuh ort tuh be a—!"

"*Basta*—enough!" snarled the Bandit sternly. "Where is that damn Sheriff?"

"He's out huntin' yuh, I reckon," George grunted. But he was not over his mad yet. He added vindictively, "An' when he ketches up with yuh, I shore hope he boils yuh in lard! You sure got yore guts criticizin' my poetry! It's made the best crowned heads of You-rope laff!"

"I guess so!" remarked the man with the gun. "That stuff would make a pall-bearer laff! Now listen—" he cautioned gruffly. "You tell that slat-sided Ten-Hawse squirt that if he don't keep his long nose outa my business, I'm goin' t' bend my gun across his haid—an' that goes for you, too! I'm gettin' tired of bein' run all round Robin Hood's barn. This chasin' round has got t' stop!—*Understand?* Next time I see that nitwit on my trail, I'm goin' t' make buzzard bait outa him—git me?"

George nodded. But he wasn't trembling any

longer. A savage resentment had him in its grip, and he was beyond the restraint of caution. "Yuh think yo're some pumpkins, I reckon; stickin' up these stages an' all. But yuh're sure ridin' fer a fall. A guy that turns up his nose at the kinda verse I write is jest plain too dang smart fer his britches—an' that applies tuh *you!* I'm goin' tuh camp on yore trail—"

"Huh! You an' who else?"

"Jest me an' Ten-Hawse Jones! We're goin tuh make you hard tuh ketch!"

"I'll be hard t' catch, all right," the Bandit sneered. "You tell this girl-stealin' Sheriff if he makes one more move in my direction, it'll surer'n hell be his last one! An' you tell him t' steer plumb clear of Tony Sumptor or I'll collect enough of his hide t' make a saddle cover. Throw over that hawg-laig, now—an' be dang careful how you do it."

George took his gun gingerly from the holster and slithered it across the floor.

The Bandit left it where it lay. But suddenly his gun spat fire in three loud blasts. The lamp went out and George was left alone, staring at a slice of star-filled sky revealed by the open door.

XIX

The Baited Trap

Ten-Horse Jones returned next day at noon. He turned his remuda into the public corral and clumped into the Alamo Restaurant, where he stayed for some forty-five minutes. When he came out there was a peculiar glint in his eye and he headed directly for his office.

George met him at the door with a hearty greeting. "I got some news fer yuh, boy—C'mon in an' close the door. Dang wind gits colder ever' minute. Was that driver dead?"

"Dead!" growled Ten-Horse, planting both hands on his hips and glaring. "Dead—hell, yes! An' planted ten prayers deep! The fall broke his neck like a pipestem; that cliff where he went off the road's near sixty feet from the floor of the canyon. I hear you been doin' some shootin' last night," he added grimly, pulling off his gloves. "Six diff'rent fellas give me six diff'rent accounts! What in hell was goin' on?"

"Wal," said George uneasily, "I'll tell yuh."

And he did so. "That black-browed polecat told me to tell yuh that yuh better quit chasin' him around, if yuh value yore health; an' tuh steer plumb clear of Tony Sumptor!" He eyed the sheriff curiously.

"George," said Ten-Horse soberly, "do you think that fella was Slow Jim?"

"I dunno," George scowled. "Voice seemed kinda famil'ar-like, sometimes; but I'd hate tuh swear it was or it wasn't. In a case like that, voices can be dang misleadin'. But one thing's certain—whoever this Bandit is, he sure has got it in fer yuh. An' fer me, too, seems like. It looks tuh me like we jest got tuh git busy, Sheriff."

"Oh, it does, does it!" Ten-Horse blared. "Hell's unvarnished hinges! What in blue blazes do you think I *been* doin'? But you ain't missed the nail completely—*you're* goin' t' git busy dang pronto! I been hearin' a few things about you—'bout how you been tellin' folks that if *you* was sheriff there'd be a diff'rent story told. There'd be a diff'rent story, all right—an' there's goin' t' be one anyhow. Hereafter, my friend, you are goin' t' do some *work!*"

George sighed. "The evil thet men do lives after 'em," he quoted dolefully. "Seems like ever' time I open my mouth some dang fool sticks the wrong words into it. But I can explain—"

"Don't bother," Ten-Horse warned. "I'm goin' t' give you a chance t' prove them words."

George's blue eyes flew wide. "Y'ain't quittin', are yuh?"

"No!" snarled Jones, "I ain't quittin'! I don't

152

never quit—not till the last bean's shot from the cylinder. An' you better not try quittin', neither, or I'll make you hard to find. From here on out I'm goin' t' have teamwork—savvy? The up-bound stage is due in fifteen minutes. An' when it leaves, you're goin' out on it!"

"Who—*me?*" George scowled. "I don't wanta go no place."

"You're goin' all the same. You're goin' out with that stage as shotgun guard—somethin' I hear you been tellin' they're a long time needin'!"

"Now, listen, Ten-Hawse," George said placatingly; "I was on'y foolin'. I was on'y tryin' t' uphold the dignity of this office—"

"You'll uphold it a dang sight better sittin' on the box with a shotgun," grunted Ten-Horse, no whit relenting. He took a murderous-looking sawed-off from the cupboard and placed it in George's reluctant hands. "There'll be a diff'rent story told next time that swivel-eyed joker stops the stage!"

And to all George's cunningly-concocted alibis Ten-Horse turned a deaf ear. He remained adamant. George could as soon have moved Eagle Mountain from its rockpile base as to sway Ten-Horse from his just decision. "You been blowin', George," he told him, "an' now you got t' pay for it."

And without more ado he left the office. But he was back inside immediately.

George had heard him hail some passing walker. Now he said to George: "I want some coöperation. I'm goin' t' put a spike in some-body's gun or know the reason why! Ol' Man Sumptor's on his way over here—I just gave him the high sign. After he's been here a few minutes I'm goin' t' git away on some excuse or other, an' while I'm gone you start some of your famous reminiscin' an' let drop that dope about the Bar X herd. Use a little tact. Whatever you do, don't spoil the show—unless I miss my guess, when Sumptor learns about them cattle headin' for Mexico, hell's goin' t' git right up on its hind laigs an' howl!"

So, when Sumptor came in a moment later, Jones was busily sorting papers at his desk. "Take a seat," he called without glancing up. "Be with you in a second."

Sumptor said, "I'll stand. An'," he added pointedly, "I ain't got much time to spare, so if you got somethin' you're figgerin' t' chin about, you better git busy pronto."

Laying his papers down, Ten-Horse looked up with a scowl. "So that's the attitude you're takin', is it? Let me tell you somethin', Mister—names an' political influence don't mean a thing in my young life. I deal jest like I'm given; an' if you wanta slip a joker in the deck, don't kick if you lose the pot."

And, with a final hard glance, he returned his attention to his papers.

But not for long. With a curse, Sumptor said: "What the hell is this, anyway? You're makin' a big 'nough fool of yoreself over that Bandit without antagonizin' leadin' citizens. If you got anythin' t' say t' me, *say* it!"

Ten-Horse twisted his torso and gave the ranchman a long, cold stare. "So you don't like the way I'm conductin' the office, eh?" he purred. "Well, that's jest too bad. I guess you'd like it better, mebbe, if that McCash pelican you got roddin' your spread was packin' this star—or your friend Kinch Lee! Well, lemme tell you somethin', Sumptor; you better cut loose of them two hombres 'fore you find yourself tarred with the same brush."

With which remark Jones got to his feet and, putting on his hat, started for the door. "Keep your eye on this gentleman, George. I'll be comin' right back." And he went out the door before Sumptor could recover from surprise.

"Er—do yuh like poetry, Mister Sumptor?" George enquired.

"Poetry!" Sumptor snorted. "Ain't got no time fer it!" he growled. "An' if that young whipper-snapper thinks I'm goin' t' sit here coolin' my heels till he gits back, he's got another think!"

"Yuh better stick around a spell," George pronounced as the rancher started for the door. "He's got a warrant—"

"What!" Sumptor stopped dead in his tracks

155

and whirled round with a curse. "A warrant! You mean t' say that fool has got a warrant out fer *me?*"

George swallowed uncomfortably as he met Sumptor's outraged glare. "Wal," he murmured, "I don't know's it's fer you—but he sure has got a warrant fer someone. Was I you, I b'lieve I'd wait."

"Why, that damn fool! I'll hev his star fer this!" the rancher raged. "He can't run me around like a low *pelado* Mexican! By Gawd, there's a law in this man's country—an' I know how t' use it!"

"If youh're referrin' tuh that *abogado* Mex, why Jones has already read a riot act on *him*. That fella ain't goin' tuh be in no position tuh do anybody any good directly." He rasped a hand across his bristly jaw; tugged at his mustache. "Nope; yuh might's well set a spell an' take the weight off tired feet. Did yuh hear," he asked more cheer-fully, "about them beeves—?"

"I ain't got no time t' be talkin' cattle," Sumptor snapped. A heavy man, he was; with big, rolling shoulders and a sure, hard way. Just now his fat, roan cheeks showed anger and a gathered impatience that had almost reached the action stage. "What I wanta know," he rasped, "is why did that damn fool call me over here?"

He glared at George as though by his show of rage to force the secret from him.

But George was ready. "I can't imagine," he

said perplexedly, "unless it was about them Bar X cattle—"

"*What* Bar X cattle?"

"Why, that beef cut Lee lost haff a dozen nights ago—the one they give Tucker Hart that necktie social fer," George said, as though Sumptor were well acquainted with the circumstances.

"What about it?" the rancher gruffed suspiciously.

"Why . . . don't yuh recollect how Lee got up at the inquest an' swore them cattle had been *stole?*"

George's squint was innocence personified.

Yet a kind of cloud ran its gloom across the rancher's shaved-hog features, and a caution began to show in his watchful gaze.

But only for a moment. His shoulders stirred impatiently. "What of it?"

"Wal, nothin', much, I reckon; only some fella Ten-Hawse knows, saw that cut a couple days ago. Down below the Van Horn Mountains. They was bein' drifted—"

"Of course," cried Sumptor; "an' that proves it! Some of Hart's ol' gang is runnin' 'em into Mexico!"

"Ten-Hawse—he's got a diff'rent notion, seems like. Yuh see," George added confidentially, "them cattle was bein' drifted by Kinch Lee's range boss, Gates."

It was great bait.

Sumptor's jaw dropped open. He closed it with

a snap of teeth and never said a word. But his eyes gleamed wickedly as he sloshed his hat upon his head.

He went out like the wrath of God.

XX

Dahlmer Lays the Law Down

When he hustled from the Sheriff's Office, Ten-Horse was thinking about his plot to trap the Lazy D rancher—and praying it would work. Too long by far had he been working blind; he was determined now that if he couldn't get a lead any other way, he was fully justified in striving to get one through strategy.

He was thinking also—and bitterly—about the Bandit's presumptuous order that he 'steer clear of Tony Sumptor.' That guy had plenty brass! If nerve were doughnuts, that stage-robbing pilgrim would have enough to start in business! he reflected. And if it *was* Slow Jim who was responsible for all these stick-ups and stabbings, then it was time Slow Jim got his mortal tintype blasted!

Friendship could only go so far—and Ten-Horse figured his had been plenty stretched. It was all well and good to stick up for a guy and live according to the Golden Rule; but when the guy started ramming his foot down your throat, it was time to bite some toes off! "In the words of that jasper, Shakespeare," Ten-Horse muttered, "when your one-time pardner is figurin' on crawlin' outa the country like a whipped cur—or is tryin' to give out that impression so's he can go round stickin' Bowie-knives in people—it's high time fer friendship t' be pullin' in its horns!"

So when he saw Tony Sumptor sitting in her father's touring car a few blocks down the street, he felt no shame in hurrying that way pronto. He'd given Jim fair warning; if the fellow didn't care enough about her to stick around, that was *his* tough luck. He, Ten-Horse Jones, believed in making hay while the sun shone—and in patching up an apparent misunderstanding while a girl's old man was busy someplace else!

And he lost no time in starting negotiations.

"Howdy, Tony!" he grinned, pulling off his tall black Stetson. "You git prettier every day! By gosh, I'll bet you're the most perfectest specimen of female pulcritood in forty-eight localities! How's your father feelin' these days?"

"Why don't you ask him?" she said coolly. "He just stepped into your office."

"Shucks," Ten-Horse said, "I didn't come over here t' talk about that gentleman. I was figurin' t' make a little chin-music 'bout you an' me. I reckon," he suggested, eying her judiciously, "you're still feelin' some riled with me."

"Then you reckon," she mimicked, "plumb right!" And she returned his stare indignantly.

She was a tall and willowy creature, with long slim legs and chestnut curls. Her dark, full, lustrous eyes were brown, and topped by brows of penciled regularity. Her hair was like rubbed copper where the sunlight struck across it; but the light of her eyes was cold and scathing.

"Now, listen," Ten-Horse pleaded; "I was thinkin' about somethin' else when I bumped into you the other evenin'. Gosh, give a guy a break, can't you? I was full up to my Adam's apple with sheriff's business when you gave me the high sign the other night—cripes, if you had this job you'd be wearin' a scowl like the Grand Canyon, too!"

"At least, I'd be polite enough to *speak* to my friends when I saw them," she stated. "Or . . . perhaps you don't consider me one of your friends any more?"

"Shucks, I 'low you know a heap better'n that," Ten-Horse defended. "But honest now—ain't you engaged to Slow Jim Hart?"

"Certainly *not!*"

"Oh! Say—that's *swell!* cried Ten-Horse enthusiastically. "Mean t' say you're open to bids—no *kiddin'?*"

"What do you think I am?" she cried indignantly. "A—a poker pot? Or a *horse?*" Her delectable little mouth began to quiver. "Oh, dear!" she exclaimed, and tears abruptly spilled across her lashes.

Ten-Horse stood there dumbly, twirling his battered hat.

She gulped, "I don't ever want to see another man as long as I live! I'm—I'm going to shut myself up in a convent and become a—a nun!"

Ten-Horse gasped. "You *wouldn't!* Good Lord, Tony; you can't mean that!"

"Yes, I can—I *do!*" she blinked, and dabbed at her eyes with a filmy bit of cloth no bigger than a sparrow's diaper. "This country's no fit place for a trusting girl. I—"

Ten-Horse glared. "Who's the guy? Slow Jim? What's that damn fool done?" he gritted fiercely.

"Now, isn't that just like a man! *Done!* Hasn't he rolled up his tail and gone sneaking out of the country? Then why do you stand there asking me what he's done?" she wailed. "Don't you think that's quite enough?"

The sheriff's face dropped like a cake. "Oh," he muttered lugubriously. "Then you *was* figuring on marryin' him, after all."

"I was *considering* it," she corrected tartly.

"Uh-huh." Ten-Horse made marks in the dust with the toe of one boot, and eyed them moodily. "Yeah, I see. I expect you'd like for me t' haul him back, eh?"

"Indeed not!"

"But," Ten-Horse protested; "you said—"

161

"Well, you never had gumption enough to propose yourself! I can't wait around forever, can I? A girl has to think of the future these days. Nobody wants to die an *old maid!*"

Ten-Horse was staring at her open-mouthed. "Huh?" he gulped. *"Say that again!"*

"You'd better get along about your business," she told him primly. "Everyone around here's staring at us. Do please go, Ten-Horse—do you want to make a *scene?* Look at Jed Thompson grinning! And that hateful Arnold person—I just know he's making up some joke about us!"

Ten-Horse didn't give a hoot for the scene—or for the smirking townsmen, either. But as he twisted his head around to look, he spied Tumbleweed Sumptor coming from the Sheriff's Office, and decided that a quick retreat was indicated.

There were times when discretion *was* the better part of valor—and this was definitely one of them!

"All right," he grumbled, "I'll clear out. But first chance I get, I'm comin' out t' see you—an' I'll be bringin' somethin' to go on that purty hand!"

From the barroom of the Striped Tiger he watched Tumbleweed Sumptor climb into the machine, and the way he slammed the door was certainly a portent. The old man's foot crunched the starter like it was a rattlesnake. The engine woke up with a roar, and a minute later there was nothing to be seen of the old crate but a dust cloud in the distance.

Ten-Horse moved to the bar like a man in a dream. He ordered three fingers neat, and downed it like a glass of water. He took a second and stowed it just as easy.

The barkeep scratched his head. "You ain't been playin' in hard luck, hev ye? Ain't lost yer job or nothin'?"

Ten-Horse came out of his reverie. "Huh? No —hell, no! I jest got engaged to the best dang filly that ever trod the Great Staked Plains!"

"A *hawse?*" The bartender's eye bugged out.

"No!" blared Ten-Horse; "a girl, doggone yuh! An' prettier'n a twenty-mule borax team! She's got a voice like temple chimes an' a shape that would pull a blind man forty miles!"

The barkeep shrugged. "That's what they all say," he grunted skeptically. "But when you been married much as I hev, you'll learn t' take em with a bag of salt—epsom preferred. Wait'll you git hitched up an' then that temple voice'll sound like hell emigratin' on cartwheels. You won't git no bill-an'-cooin' then; it'll be Ten-Horse this, an' Ten-Horse that; an' Ten-Hawse, will you fetch in the lumber fer that shelf you was aimin' to fix las' August? An' Ten-Hawse, will you mind the kids while I take in a pitcher show? Don't talk t' *me* about these women, 'cause you're talkin' to a man what knows!"

"What's been eatin' on *you?*" Ten-Horse grinned. "What you need's a snort of rye. Here, have one on me—an' fill me up another while you're at it. This must be new stuff. Never tasted anythin' that good in *here* before."

"There comes that deputy of yours."

"C'mon up here, George, an' help me celebrate," called Ten-Horse heartily. "I've just got engaged to the finest little woman in the world!"

"Yeah?" George sniffed. "Who is she, if I might ask?"

"Tony Sumptor! By cripes, a fella never knows his luck!"

George looked at him. "Humph," he grunted. "I expect it's jest as well."

Where was a clatter of wheels and a pounding of hoofs and the stage pulled up with a flourish just across the street.

"You better leave philosophy alone an' drink your liquor," Ten-Horse observed. "Because you've got a date on that hearse with a sawed-off shotgun, an' you sure better look like goin'."

"Aw—hell," George muttered disconsolately. "Listen tuh reason—"

"If I listened to reason I'd fire you," Ten-Horse told him, "so you just rustle on down to the office an' take that shotgun for a ride."

Ten-Horse set down his glass and turned reluctantly as someone touched him on the arm. It was Edson J. Dahlmer, the friendly County Com. —only just now Dahlmer's friendliness appeared a little out at the elbows. But Ten-Horse made out like he didn't notice. "Howdy, Ed!" he said with a stab at being jovial.

Dahlmer made no such stab. His nod was brief and non-committal. And the eye that flicked to the half-full glass still encircled by Jones' left hand was cold. "Got out that reward notice on young Hart yet?"

"Well, no . . . not yet," Ten-Horse admitted.

"Thought not." Dahlmer put the flats of his hands upon his hips and the frost in his glance almost crackled. "I guess you've got that menace from Bloody Run under lock an' key by now, though, ain't you?"

"No," scowled Jones; "not yet."

The County Commissioner's eyebrows went up three wrinkles. "I'm surprised to find you hittin' the booze in here, then," he remarked. "Seems to me that if I were in your boots I'd be spendin' my time to more advantage. What have you been doin' to justify your wages?"

"What is this—a inquisition?" Jones demanded.

"It's a check-up," Dahlmer answered. "An' I'm bound to tell you that what I find ain't to my likin'. I'm disappointed in you, Jones. When we put you into office we figured you'd take the job serious an' get this county cleaned up. On the contrary, we find that things are getting steadily worse."

"If you don't like my style," began Ten-Horse hotly, "you can—"

"It isn't a question of style. What we're after are results. An' frankly, Jones it looks to us like you been playin' politics. We—"

"Politics!" Ten-Horse burst out furiously. "I ain't had no time t' play anythin'—let alone *politics!* All I been doin' is latherin' up my horses chasin' after that gosh-blamed stick-up! An' what time I ain't been doin' that, I been sweatin' my shirts out tryin' t' git the low-down on Dunkett's killer an' the bunch that swung Tucker Hart! I've missed meals right an' left, worked like a dawg, an' gone without my sleep more'n haff the time! Now, if you don't like my style you can take your blasted job an' shove it up the rainspout!"

Dahlmer's smile was thin. "It's not a question," he said, "of what I like. It's the job of the County Commissioners to see that you get results; or, if you don't, to get a man who will. We got to keep the taxpayers satisfied an' see that they get a run for their money. They expect to see some action. You been chargin' 'em right an' left for posses that never catch anything but colds.

"Now, take this Bandit of Bloody Run. Besides the general hell he's been raisin', he's killed two men—one of 'em an important person, an' grabbed thirty thousand in minted gold bein' sent to the Del Rio Bank. Have you got a reward out for him yet?"

166

"I got one bein' printed—sure."

"Bein' printed? What's the printer doin'—makin' special type?"

"Fer all I know, he's been makin' whoopee with the hotel-keeper's daughter!" Ten-Horse snarled. "What do yuh take me for—a regiment? I can't keep my eye on everything!"

"Well, you hustle him up. How much reward you offerin'?"

"One hundred bucks—"

"That ain't enough. Make it five. Nobody's goin' t' run their broncs to skin an' bones on the off chance of gettin' a cut on a hundred dollars! Boost the price an' cut down on your posses; that way you'll get half the county workin' for nothing an' the tax-payers won't have no kick. What's that deputy of yours been doin' with his time? From all I hear, all he does is wear out the seat of his pants wrastlin' with some damfool poetry! What kind of a occupation's that for a grown-up man? Is the fella simple?"

"That fella," snarled Ten-Horse Jones, "is settin' shotgun guard on the up-bound stage this minute! If he writes poetry in his spare time, it's no skin off'n *my* nose—nor yours, either!"

"You be careful how you talk," Edson J. Dahlmer glared, "or you won't have nothin' *but* spare time on *your* hands, young man! Now you get out a flyer on that Bandit, an' one on—"

"Say! Who's runnin' this office?" Jones

demanded. "Me, or the County Commissioners?"

"You are, but—"

"Then never mind the buts! When I want any advice from you, I'll ask fer it! Until then, as long as I'm packin' this star I'll git along without your help!"

The County Com. was white to the lips. "Don't go too far, Mister Jones," he growled. "There's no man so hell's-fire good he can't be replaced! You get out that flyer on the Bandit pronto, an' get one out on Slow Jim Hart before the sun goes down tonight, or I'll be round to collect that badge—"

"You an' who else?" bellowed Ten-Horse belligerently.

"Just me *alone*." Dahlmer smiled with his teeth and stalked off down the street.

XXI

"Why, You Meechin' Yaller Hound!"

From a corner table a man looked up and laughed. It was Bill McCash, and red rimmed his eyes from the rotgut he had drunk.

"You laughin' at *me?*" blared Ten-Horse, balling up his fists.

"I wa'n't laffin' at yore uncle!" the Lazy D foreman sneered.

What Ten-Horse might have done had he not been interrupted will probably never be known. But at that instant the batwing doors swung open and a man lurched in, gawped around, and shoved back through the swinging doors.

There was a clatter of hoofs, a neigh of mingled fear and protest, and then the man reappeared, backing through the batwings and pulling with vigorous curses on some taut-stretched reins.

The man was Shorty Hebron and he was drunk.

"C'mon in here, dang yuh!" he grunted through the panting of his labor. "C'mon in outa the cold! D'yuh wanta git new-*monia*? F' Cri-shakes! Yuh can't expect this barkeep t' bring yuh drink out there!"

More cursing, panting, and tugging abruptly introduced a horse's head between the slatted doors.

It was George's steed, Dynamite, and his bared teeth and rolling eyes plainly signified his desire to stay outside.

But Shorty was adamant. "C'min yere, dang yuh! Whashyuh think thish is—*a tug o' war?* Dad-burn it, yuh embarrassh me! I never had no pal refush t' drink with me before!"

"Now, listen!" the barman said, plainly getting riled. "You can't bring that hawse in here, Shorty! 'Tain't yore hawse, anyway—yuh want t' git hung fer a hawse-thief?"

"Who in blazes you callin' a hawsh-thief?" growled Shorty, letting go the reins with a suddenness that left the straining pony with its head wedged firmly between the doors.

"Who you callin' a hawsh-thief?" he repeated, pivoting with the extreme dignity of his condition and eying the barkeep sternly. He dropped a belligerent hand to the gun protruding from his chaps. "Why, you onregenerate back-country Mormon! Eat them words or I'll break every glassh in thish joint!"

Ten-Horse strode hurriedly forward. "Shucks, Shorty," he cried, grabbing the irate puncher's arm; "don't pay no attention t' him—he's jest talkin' to hear his head rattle. C'mon up to the bar an' have a drink. I just got engaged to the most beautiful gal in forty-eight nations—I call that somethin' t' celebrate; don't you?"

"I dunno," muttered Shorty. "That dependsh. Whosh 'er ol' man?"

"Your boss," said Ten-Horse. "Tumbleweed Sumptor."

"Great guns!" exclaimed Shorty, and shook his head. He looked at the sheriff aghast, then shook his head again. "Wal," he mumbled, "I reckon yuh're more t' be pitied than shenshured."

"Shucks," said Ten-Horse sagely. "A man's a fool t' live a single life."

"An' a bigger fool ef he doesn't," declared the puncher, wagging his head. "But you don't git the point—et al, as they shay in the booksh. A fella who'd pick that ol' wallaper fer a in-law shore ish askin' fer grief—an'll git it!"

Ten-Horse laughed. "I ain't marryin' her ol' man," he pointed out. "C'mon, let's have a drink."

"I'll be the one t' treat, then. What'll yuh hev?"

"Make mine a Scotch an' soda," McCash said, getting up.

Ten-Horse swung a wicked glare. "I've stood all your didoes I've a mind to. You keep outa this 'fore you git hurt!"

"You don't look so tough t' me! Where d'you bury yore daid?"

"Jest keep right on an' you'll find out! I chucked you outa *one* place, an' I can jes' as easy chuck you outa *this!*"

"Yeah—" McCash sneered thinly, "—Jones, the Chucker! But two can play at *that* game, an' you ain't foolin' *me!* I sabe what you're up to! You ain't satisfied t' see Shorty wabblin' on his pins— you wanta git the brainless idjit drunker so's mebbe he'll open up an' spill the names of who hung Tucker Hart!"

There was an instant of utter silence, then Ten-Horse swore in a fury.

But the fat was in the fire and no amount of cussing would help things much. You could tell by the pale, scared look round Shorty's gills that, whatever he *might* have said—wild horses couldn't drag the information from him now!

Ten-Horse planted both brown hands on his hips and glowered. "I oughta bash yore face in!" he snarled wickedly. "I reckon if it all come out, we'd hear how *you* was pullin' on that rope as hard as any!"

McCash laughed loudly—too loudly, Ten-Horse thought, but he sobered quickly and an ugly glint got in his eyes. "Talk's cheap; but lemme tell you somethin', *hombre*—you keep foolin' round with Tony Sumptor an' I'll give you somethin' besides *talk!*"

"Why, you meechin' yaller hound!" roared Ten-Horse. "You give me any more that kinda lip an' I'll send you to the dentist t' git your bridle teeth repaired."

"You don't scare nobody with bones in his spinal column," McCash came back. "You git gay with *me* an' there won't be enough left of you t' snore!"

"Is that so!" Ten-Horse snorted insultingly, and rolled his sleeves. "I'm gonna skin you up till you look like the U.S. flag!"

"You're gonna shout, too!" jeered McCash, and went for his gun.

He was fast—but not quite fast enough.

Ten-Horse sprang with a howl of rage. His bunched left fist struck McCash like the sound of a board on water. His right, coming up from his bootstraps, took McCash in the mouth and crashed him sprawling against the bar where he hung for one taut moment, then slid glassy-eyed to the floor.

Ten-Horse blew on his bleeding knuckles and eyed the staring barman. "You got half an hour," he told him, "to close this joint. If it *ain't* closed by then—*look out!* The County Commissioners want action an' by gee I aim t' give it to 'em! An' as fer *you*," he growled, turning on the gaping Hebron, "You're due for the best cell in my cooler. An' there you're gonna stay until you open up an' talk!"

XXII

"When I Pop the Whip, You Jump!"

Cresting a wooded knoll, the dark-clothed rider pulled his black bronc to a standstill and with his left gloved hand reached swiftly out and clamped the gelding's nostrils. No sound disturbed the waiting stillness, and he sat like that without further movement for many moments while he keened the yonder murk with a need for detail. But the far high clouds did not let go their clutch on a captured moon, and all below was dark and bathed in a somber murk that disclosed little save the gaunt outlines of huddled buildings; the sand-scoured structures of the Lazy D ranch headquarters.

Nearest the moveless watcher a bunkhouse reared its sprawling form, a deeper dark against a bank of shifting shadows. The corral came next, and looked from here to be empty—distinctly a stroke of luck if Sumptor's punchers were upon the range someplace. Beyond, and a bit to the right, stood the foreman's shanty, a glimmer of light leaking from a carelessly blanketed window. And back of all these vaguely showed the squat outlines of Sumptor's 'dobe house—a place oft-visited by more than one rangeland politician.

Long and carefully the watcher surveyed these things, appearing to pay a particular attention to the clearing in the midst of which these structures stood, and staring with keenest attention toward the Stygian blackness of the long veranda, and that gloom through which the corral poles were laced with ghostly dimness.

Presently the man dismounted, leaving his sleek black horse in the clump of aspens and starting determinedly forward afoot.

Cautiously he descended the spillway of the slope, approaching closer the huddle of dried-mud buildings step by step; more than once pausing to keen the roughening wind and get his bearings.

He seemed to possess that strange sixth sense that is given to men who long have ridden the lonely trails and those which are most dimly marked. He appeared to have that intuition which warningly heralds another's coming minutes before the keenest eye could possibly perceive it, or the quickest ear have caught its beat.

Like a blind man's cane, this sense now served him well, causing him to flatten himself against the tawny earth.

And none too soon!

The ranch house door eased abruptly open. Sumptor's burly shape stood etched against lamp's brightness in the room behind. He stood there for a long-drawn moment, peering into the swirling, gusty black. Then, as suddenly, Sumptor tipped his head and wheeled away, slamming the door hard shut against the wind.

The black-garbed watcher started to his feet. He was halfway up when a shift in the draft rising off the sage flung a muffled, rhythmic pound of hoofs against his ears.

It dropped him flat, that sound; dropped him flat and held him moveless, with his chest against the cracked and parching gumbo with his breath held taut and one eye cocked toward that place where the oncoming rider soon must show.

And then a horse came rocketing from the murk. A rider hit dirt on skidding bootheels—came lurching forward in a staggering run, stiff-legged from jolting contact with the saddle.

The ranch house door flung open, spilling its bar of light across the yard, and illumining for one brief moment the masklike face of Deuces Darst.

175

The unseen watcher slowly came to his feet, his eyes upon the gambler and a look of satisfaction about his grim-lipped mouth.

"Where he stood in deepest shadow, this man was not picked out by any faintest radiance from that yonder open door, yet he could see both Sumptor and the gambler plainly. Darst was moving toward the house.

The black-garbed rider moved forward sound-less as a cat, each springy stride inexorably cutting down the distance between himself and Darst. With quick and wraithlike stealth he came to the pole enclosure, pausing beside its bars and sinking to a crouch, discernible only as one more dense shape among the shifting blot of shadows.

He stayed like a halted tumbleweed against those cold peeled poles until Darst joined the rancher in the doorway. Then, just as he prepared to shorten the remaining distance, another door was opened.

It was the door of the foreman's shanty, and the spilled light crossing the porch showed Bill McCash with a strange expression on his face, intently staring toward the house.

The men had passed inside, but the door was still ajar, and in its refracted radiance the gambler's horse was plainly seen.

A muffled oath burst from the range boss. He shut his door with a bootheel and with hand on gun started forward across the yard.

A malicious grin curled the mouth of the hidden watcher.

Then he, too, started forward.

Deuces Darst abruptly wheeled and closed the door. "No need advertisin' this visit." His words were rough, but the masklike set of his pallid features remained the same and gave no inkling of the thoughts passing through his narrow head. He dropped the bar in its slot and put his back against it. "Dang lucky I got a hunch an' fogged on over here," he said, looking meaningly at Kinch Lee where he sat in Sumptor's rocker.

"You don't proddy to get need to," grumbled the Bar X owner sullenly. "I didn't come here 'cause I like the climate or the brand of hospitality. I come because the ol' man sent fer me."

Darst eyed Sumptor curiously. "Still worryin' over that Dunkett knifing?"

Sumptor's heavy eyebrows raised. "I don't worry," he stated flatly, and contempt lay plain across his plump roan cheeks. "I leave that chore for squirts like you an' other fools that don't know better. But I'm glad you come," he added grimly. "Save me goin' over the same ground twice. Lee jest got here, an' I guess it won't hurt you to hear what I've got to tell him."

"Ahr-r-r," Lee growled. "Breath yore save to blow yore porridge. Never mind workin' up a mystery. Cut loose an' spill yore guts."

Vicious wrath rode the puckered blue gaze Sumptor wheeled upon them. "There's a belly crawlin' snake in this crowd someplace. A dirty, double-crossin' hound—an' it sure ain't me!"

Darst breathed softly. "A double-crosser, eh? Who is it?" His gambler's eyes followed Sumptor's gaze to the face of tense Kinch Lee.

Lee's loose-coupled figure stirred uneasily in the chair and his ill-matched eyes seemed to freeze and glaze as he met that concerted stare. A pink tongue slowly edged across his lips.

But he made no talk.

"Them cattle the Bar X lost—Lee's famous beef cut," Sumptor said, "is down below the Van Horn Mountains bein' drifted over towards Mexico. They're—"

Lee put up a pretty good show of surprise, cutting in: "Didn't I tell you that?"

"*No,* you didn't tell me that!" ripped Sumptor, banging his fist down on the table. "An' you had no *'tenshun* of tellin' me, neither, you mangy cur!"

Lee came out of his chair stiff-faced. "What are you tryin' t' pull here? Are you claimin', by Gawd, I rustled them steers myself—?"

"Damn well right I am!" Sumptor shouted. "That herd was in charge of yore foreman, Gates!"

Darst's right hand dropped swiftly to his gun.

But Lee kept his head. "Of course it was— who'd you think would be in charge of it? *Hart?*"

That brought a deeper flush across Sumptor's congested features. It stopped Darst's hand just short of his gun.

Lee said easily, "I figured this thing out with a little care. You," he recalled, looking at Sumptor, "was hellbent t' get Hart out of the way. You had that brass disc from off his chaps—recollect how you handed it to me the other day with the advice it might come in handy? I figured so, too; an' pretty soon I saw how we could use it. I staged that fake raid. But I wasn't fool enough to leave them steers around where pryin' eyes might get a look at 'em. I told Gates to haze 'em down south of the Van Horns for a spell till this thing sort of cooled over, or we got a chance to sell 'em to good advantage. Market's lousy right now, anyhow."

"Them cattle," Sumptor said, not quite satisfied, "belong to *me*. You had a lot of guts drivin' 'em over the country without my say-so. An'," he added harshly, "I ain't convinced yet you wasn't figgerin' to sell 'em an' pocket the change if you got the chance."

"Think what you want," Lee shrugged. "I've told you how it was. A man don't expect a feller that would see his brother hangin' to a cotton-wood t' have much faith in others."

Sumptor's roan cheeks went dark and he took a half step forward.

But Darst said quickly: "Brother? Who—*Hart?* What's he talkin' about?"

"Where the hell you been hidin' all your life?" Lee sneered.

But Sumptor swung his shaved-hog features with an oath. "You rubbed out that Hart whelp yet?"

"No, I ain't," Darst answered. "An' what's more, I don't know as I will. I'm gettin' a little tired of pullin' your chestnuts outa the fire. I've done this much, though; I've tried ribbin' Ten-Horse into jailin' him. I ain't—"

"No—I'll bet you ain't!" Sumptor finished nastily. "All you're good for is settin' round some table with a deck of pasteboards an' a pile of borrowed money! When it come t' doin' a growed man's work, you're sure some short of reach!"

"An' why?" Darst lashed with glittering eyes. "Because I ain't been gettin' my cut—"

"*What* cut?" Sumptor exploded.

"You know damn' well what cut!" snarled Darst belligerently. "My cut on them cattle you been rustlin' for the last four years—them cattle I been findin' you a market for! That's what!"

He glowered at Sumptor with a plain emotion. "You divide that swag you've tucked away an' you'll get a lot more cooperation from the rest of us! We ain't in this for our health!"

The room was illumined by a pair of kerosene lamps. Their yellow light showed the fury on Sumptor's face . . . and the ham-like hands that at the ends of his hairy arms looked more like murderous clubs than human fists. With a vicious kick he booted a clod of dried mud skuttering across the room. He strode deliberately to Darst and stood there glaring with his bare-lipped face almost touching the gambler's own.

"*I'll* decide," he gritted, "when these cuts are goin' t' be made!" And one fist jumped out and smashed Darst back against the wall before the gambler could flip a finger. "*I'm* running this show—*get me?* An' when my style don't suit, you can cut for other timber!"

Darst's taut face was sheetlike in its whiteness. With lips that hardly moved, he said: "I'm stickin' right here till I get my cut—"

"*Yore* cut! Why, you saddle-blanket card sharp! You ain't *got* no cut save by my grace! You don't think yore one-hawse politics is worth a damn t' *me,* do you?"

A feline glitter streaked Darst's dark eyes. "Jest the same, I'm stickin' till I get my cut," he repeated stubbornly.

"Then," Sumptor told him with a thin-lipped grin, "you'll be round here quite a spell! Now get this straight—I want Hart's lamp snuffed *pronto!* I got my reasons an' they're plenty good. He's found out—"

"I don't give a damn what he's found," Darst purred. "All I'm lookin' out for is t' get my slice of that swag you been pilin' up. An' believe me,

I'm goin' to get it." His look was on Sumptor wickedly. "You promised—"

"You shut yore goddam trap an' keep it shut!" Sumptor roared. He smashed the table with his clenched right fist. "I'll do the talkin' here. When yore advice is wanted, you'll hear me askin' for it—an' when you do, it'll sure be one sorry day!

"You're no more use to me than Lee. An' I guess you jest as lieve pull some fast stuff if you thought that you could cut it. Why didn't you lead Jim Hart when he come walkin' into yore office the other night? Why—"

"There's others beside young Hart that are gettin'—"

"*I'm* doin' the talkin' here! Why didn't you blast Hart when he follered you into the Sheriff's Office last night? You'll never get a better chance than you had ready-made when them lights went out! You better swap them fancy duds for a pair o' jeans an' git yoreself out on the range where yuh can earn the wage I'm payin' you! That damn Striped Tiger joint ain't worth haff o' what it's costin' me—"

"It served all right for me to get you buyers for that rustled stock, though, didn't it?" Darst sneered. "Now you've decided t' turn respectable, I guess the ol' crowd ain't good enough for you—"

Sumptor's fist drove him back against the wall. Twice that ham-like mauler that was Sumptor's fist lashed out; and each time it struck, the report was like a distant pistol shot.

He backed off and Darst stood there spitting blood.

"You got enough?" he jeered, wheeling round to where he could watch Lee, too. "Or shall I feed you some more?"

The gambler's slit-eyed glance was baleful, and when he spoke it was through the crimsoning handkerchief he was holding to his battered lips. "I'll make you sweat for that, Sumptor."

Sumptor's bull-throated laughter made the cross-beams ring.

"Seems to me," Lee murmured, "we got enough on our hands without fightin' amongst ourselves. You found out," he queried of Sumptor, "who that Bandit fella is?"

"Don't go worryin' 'bout that Bandit," the rancher sneered. "He'll be taken care of when the time comes. Long's he keeps his nose outa *my* game, I don't give a hoot about him. Let Jones worry about him—that's what he's gettin' paid for. Lee, you get me a bill o' sale to the Hart place. I want it by tomorrow night."

Lee scowled. "I should think," he said, "the Bandit was more important to us right now than that muckin' ranch—"

"I'll do the thinkin' for this bunch," Sumptor stated. "That Bandit may seem important to you an' Darst, but what *I* want is title to the Hart ranch—an' I'm expectin' you t' get it for me. That clear?"

Lee nodded sullenly.

"I guess you think," Darst sneered, "that since the Bandit's after *my* scalp first, your own'll be safe indefinitely. You might be due for a little surprise."

Sumptor eyed him sharply. Then he sneered. "Some more of yore damn melodrammer, I suppose." He watched Lee go back to the rocker, ignoring Darst completely. He took a turn or two about the room. He stopped and faced them, his back against the mantel.

"Slow Jim's got to go," he muttered finally. "An' I'll tell you why. Slow Jim's found out somethin' his ol' man never had the sense t' guess—the relationship between you whelps an' me. He's found it out, an' we got to close his mouth before he starts in yappin'. Pity Tucker couldn't 'a' recognized me for the brother he left t' rot in a damn Mex prison twenty years back— I'd like t' seen the stinker's face when he found it out . . . if he ever did! Left me t' die like a rat in that dungeon; his own brother, curse 'im; he wouldn't left a blasted finger! I swore then I'd get him; an' I did.

"Now look—I'm respected round this country, an' I aim t' stay that way. I don't want no damn kinship ribbed 'tween you two birds an' me. *Understand?* Slow Jim'll talk jest as quick as he gets ready—it's you fellas' job t' plant him 'fore that time comes."

"If he's been keepin' still," Darst said, "chances are he'll go right on keepin' still—"

"Yeah, that's jest the kinda remark I'd expect from a fool like you!" Sumptor's roan cheeks darkened. "Why, that cur's been playin' round with 'Tonia! I won't hev it! Even if he'd keep his talk to himself, I still don't want him round. I got other plans fer that girl. By Gawd, you fellas want t' bump him quick!"

"You got more damn gall!" Darst snarled. "Go out an' do your own killin'—ain't nobody sittin' on *your* shirttail!"

"No?" Sumptor's eyes squeezed down to slits. "You'll both do like I say or you'll never touch one penny of that loot—*hear me? When I pop the whip, you jump!*"

Darst strode over to the table, brushed off a pile of litter, and commenced laying out a game of Klondike. But Kinch Lee scowled like the information had soured his stomach.

Sumptor's words cut like a dull knife across this silence. "I got a pretty good list of the things you birds have done in the last few years . . . got 'em all down on paper—includin' that bank robbery the two of you nearly fizzled las' fall. Got it all writ out on paper—an' put where you can't get yore hands within a mile of it!"

He eyed them, gloating. "Double-cross me, my

185

buckos, an' you'll both hang higher than a kite!"

He stared at them from under his shaggy brows; searchingly, knowingly, maliciously. "Yeah, you hate my guts," he said. "But you'll do what I tell yuh, because you don't either of yuh trust the other; an' it'll take the both of you, an' more besides, t' get the best of Tumbleweed Sumptor. You'll take my orders or go to hell on shutters!"

Darst and Kinch Lee eyed each other, covertly and with speculation. But it had always been like Sumptor said; they'd never gotten along and probably never would. So now they eyed each other and wondered—wondered where all this hate and suspicion could end.

Sumptor yanked the cork from a bottle and drank deeply, but with his evil puckered eyes alert, and with his cold glance never leaving them.

When he put the bottle down he got to his feet and stood there eying them with his smug and hateful smile.

"I guess, Kinch, you better be sendin' a man down into that Van Horn country with word for Gates to start them cattle back. You'll be rememberin' you've only been handlin' them critters on shares; they're mine, an' I like t' have my cattle where I can look 'em over when the notion hits me. 'Course, there's other ways fer me t' get 'em, whether you send a man or not. But I wouldn't be wantin' t' have t' prosecute one of my own boys fer cattle stealin', now would I?"

XXIII

Pony George
Displays His Mettle

The shank of afternoon was wheeling round, the horses were crawling up a steeply winding pitch, and Pony George—a cud of the driver's prized Star Plug bulging a bristled cheek—was calling to mind sundry exploits of a highly-colored past.

"Did I tell yuh 'bout that time I pulled Red Lawler out of Turpentine Gulch? . . . Didn't? . . . Wal, son, you got a treat in store! Turpentine Gulch in them days—"

George's yarn, like the stage, came to a sudden jolting stop. Across the backs of the snorting horses his wide-eyed gaze was fixed on the unmoving figure of a horseman who sat his bronc in the very middle of the narrow road.

A rifle was loosely held in the crook of the man's left arm, and something about his pose told of a grim belief in his ability to get it quickly smoking should things not shape to his liking. Furthermore, he was clad completely in black, and that was also both the color of his horse and of the neckerchief pulled up across the lower part of his face.

It was the Bandit, and the eyes below his

hatbrim were glowing like burning coals.

It was enough to make a preacher curse, and the driver—though not a member of the clergy—did so. Then he wrapped his lines about the brake handle and hoisted both hands above his head in evidence of his peaceful purpose.

But George saw red.

This was that sneering lobo who had bearded him in the Sheriff's Office the other night and cast aspersion on his verses!

George ducked down and came up with his sawed-off shotgun, letting go both barrels.

The Bandit failed to fall—he neither reeled nor staggered. The only sound was two metallic clicks. And George realized with sinking heart that his gun had not been loaded.

Beltward jabbed his hand with the frantic speed of fear.

An oath broke from the Bandit as he whipped his rifle up. He had no time to squeeze the trigger. George's first shot went crashing through his shoulder, almost throwing him from his saddle.

George's pistol continued beating up the echoes.

But the Bandit of Bloody Run had got enough. Dropping the rifle, he whirled his horse in desperation and went pelting up the cutbank. He vanished a moment later among the trees, leaving nothing behind to mark his presence but the discarded rifle and the diminishing sound of galloping hoofs.

∙ ∙ ∙

It was after dark when the stage reached Eagle Flat.

Ten-Horse was in his office and talking to a none-too-welcome visitor. "Just what, Mister Darst, has prompted your friendly call? What ax are you figurin' on grindin' now?"

Deuces smiled his thin-lipped smile. "When I got an ax to grind," he answered, "I won't be bringin' it round to you. I just stopped in to tell you I'd bought the old Hart place. I'm having the papers recorded tomorrow morning."

Ten-Horse eyed him suspiciously. "So you've bought the spread, have you? Made a deal with Slow Jim, eh? Just when," he asked, eying the gambler with interest, "was this business hatched?"

Darst's smile was thin and watchful. "Couple nights ago," he murmured casually. "Meant to tell you 'bout it sooner, but what with all this excitement rousing up about Dunkett's death an' this Bandit's didoes, it sort of slipped my mind."

"You got a bill o' sale, I reckon?"

Darst's narrowing eyes shut off his thoughts completely. But he nodded. "Certainly," he said. "Would you care to see it?"

"Sure," said Ten-Horse bluntly. "You're damn well right I would."

Darst's lips curled. But he thrust a long pale hand in a pocket of his black frock coat and

189

produced a folded paper. "Slow Jim's own writin'," he stated, passing it to the Sheriff.

Ten-Horse looked it over. He handed it back with a scowl. "Sure looks like it," he observed reluctantly. "But lookin' like it, an' *bein'* it," he added, "ain't always quite the same."

They stood there eying each other without favor for several moments, neither man dropping his gaze before the other, and neither glance holding much charity.

Then Darst growled: "Are you insinuatin' that—"

"I'm insinuatin'," interrupted Ten-Horse brusquely, "that in this case they better be!"

Color rose to the tips of Darst's small ears. But before he could frame a come-back, the door was flung open and Pony George came barging in, a sawed-off shotgun in the crook of one arm and a rifle in the other hand.

"Got him!" George smirked lustily. "He won't be robbin' no more of them durn stages fer a while! I told yuh you was usin' the wrong technique—"

"What," grunted Jones impolitely, "are you talkin' about? An' what's the idea of packin' all that artillery?"

George drew himself up straightly and swelled his chest. "The Bandit—" he informed them with a righteous satisfaction, "—that swivel-eyed Bloody-Runner! He cracked down on the stage at Shaunicy's Knob an' I loaded him up with lead! Guess that'll change his tune some! He cleared outa there like a scorpion had crawled up his pants-laig!"

"Well, by Gawd," Ten-Horse stated, "you deserve a medal!"

But a change had come over Darst's pale face. His lips were pressed together tightly. "Who was he? Did you see his face?"

"No," George grunted, "I didn't get a look at his mug, but I perforated his shoulder, so he hadn't ort t' be too dang hard tuh find."

Some of the eager interest went out of the gambler's cheeks. "Too bad," he muttered regretfully. "I'd like to see that hellion caught."

"You'll see him caught if you stick around here long enough," Ten-Horse answered. "There ain't no man can play hell with the Hudspeth County Sheriff's Office without fetchin' up at the short end of the stick. We'll have that fella by the heels before tomorrow night—less'n he pulls his pin for other parts."

"An' I guess we'll know 'im then, all right," George added. He leaned the rifle against the desk. "He dropped this gun in his hurry."

The gambler looked at it. "Forty-five ninety." He shook his head. "That won't help much. No identifying marks an' the country's full of 'em."

George sniffed. "Mebbeso," he grunted. "But we'll ketch that fella—wait an' see. When a guy bucks up ag'in' me an' Ten-Horse Jones he's askin' fer grief—an'll git it."

XXIV

Darst Tries His Hand at Prophet

Ten-Horse turned to George as soon as the gambler left the office. "All right," he advised; "unburden yourself. What you been holdin' back, an' why?"

"*Me?*" said George, looking innocent. "What you torkin' about?"

"You know blame well," Ten-Horse accused, "that you been jest about bustin' to unload somethin' or other you wasn't wantin' that pale-faced buck t' hear! What was it? You been lookin' too pleased with yourself not to know more than you been lettin' on. Did you find out who that heller was?"

"Wal," George told him, grinning, "I didn't discover a thing I ain't admitted. But from his size an' shape an' actions I'll bet yuh anything yuh wanta name that the Bandit o' Bloody Run ain't nobody else but Bill McCash!"

"McCash!" Ten-Horse bawled, and swore. "The damn Piute! I mighta knowed it was him that was doin' all this hell-raisin' behind that daw-gone mask! Durn pussy-faced hole-in-the-ground! Wait'll I get my dew-claws on 'im! I'll teach 'im t' warn me away from Tony Sumptor!"

"Yeah," said George. "But it strikes me that it don't seem no ways likely that McCash could hop aroun' so much as this blame Bloody-Runner's been doin'. Like I said, I'm bettin' anythin' yuh wanta name that it was Bill McCash what tried tuh stick me up. *But*—how do we know that Bill's the only skunk cuttin' monkey-shines behind the safety of that get-up?"

Ten-Horse stared. "You mean mebbe there is *two* fellas wearin' them black clothes an' ridin' round on black horses?"

"Sure—why not?" said George, and lowered his voice confidentially. "This stick-up was operatin', accordin' to yore tellin', quite a spell before Ol' Man Hart was hoisted—right? . . . Wal, then why couldn't McCash be the 'riginal Bloody-Runner, an' some friend o' Hart's be goin' round in a similar get-up rubbin' out the birds that strung ol' Tucker up?"

"That," said Ten-Horse presently, "is a profound thought!"

He wrinkled his brows in reflection, scowled, and finally nodded. "I believe you've called the turn," he muttered. "Trouble is, this bird that's masqueradin' as McCash ain't likely t' know McCash is the Bloody-Runner. Looks like he'd be takin' consid'rable risk impersonatin' him thataway. An'," he added softly, "for your theory to be right, this second guy would hev to know who the Tucker Hart lynchers were."

"An' who knows," George remarked doggedly, "save Shorty Hebron an' yore boy-friend, Slow Jim Hart?"

Ten-Horse scowled. "Well, the lynchers themselves would know. But that don't get us anyplace." He pulled off his black felt hat and ran a hand through his yellow hair. "Hebron's out, an' I sure can't see Slow Jim as havin' the guts for this stunt."

"No more can I," George grunted. "But what about that wart, Jeff Morris? That guy's mean enough t' drink sheep dip!"

"No," Ten-Horse grumbled; "Morris ain't got no reason to be peeved at Hart's lynchers even if he knew 'em—which ain't likely. You're lettin' your personal animus run away with you."

George scowled. " 'F I thought you was callin' me a dirty name—"

"Skip it," Ten-Horse muttered. "If somebody's masqueradin' as the Bloody-Runner to cover himself whilst workin' a campaign of extermination 'gainst Hart's lynchers, it sure ain't Morris. An' that reminds me," he added thoughtfully. "This masked hombre has threatened t' rub out Kinch Lee, Deuces Darst, an' Tumbleweed Sumptor. So, if the rest of our figures is correct, them fellas must be the ones, includin' Snake Dunkett, that strung Hart up!"

"Now," grinned George, "we're gettin' someplace." He rubbed his chin; spat thoughtfully. "Go on from there."

"Well, that bein' the case, we know that neither Lee, Darst, nor Sumptor is the guy that's doin' this killin'. Don't forget that warnin' note somebody dropped on the floor in here the other night. Darst an' you an' me was here at the time—an' so was Slow Jim Hart. It was right after he backed outa here that some vinegarone shot the lamp out! We figured then that it was him—an' him that did the whisperin'. Dang it, George; Slow Jim might be the killer at that. It sure as hell seems logical."

"Yeah—except that he has probably left the country. Yuh don't wanta forget that angle," George reminded.

Ten-Horse sloshed on his hat. "This thing'll drive me batty yet," he muttered, heading for the door. "C'mon; let's eat."

But the door opened before they reached it. Darst stood paused in the opening, regarding them with raised eyebrows. "Goin' out, boys?"

Ten-Horse looked him over suspiciously. "You been listenin' outside that door?"

"If I was figurin' to play eavesdropper," the gambler sneered, "I could find doors a lot more profitable t' listen outside than this one."

Ten-Horse Jones looked far from convinced. "Well, what are you wantin'?" he finally said.

"It was something I'd meant to ask you when I was here before. It happens," Darst said slowly, "that I own an interest in the Striped Tiger. Your padlocking the place ain't helped my pocket-book any. Would it be too much to ask that you permit us to reopen the place if I guarantee that it's run according to your orders?"

"It sure would!" Ten-Horse growled. "That place has always been a blot on this community's character. A sinkhole of iniquity, that's what it's been. An' now I got it closed, it's goin' to stay closed."

Darst hooked his thumbs in the armholes of his fancy vest and eyed them with a suggestive smile. "It might," he hinted, "be made profitable to you was you to reconsider that decision."

"Are you tryin' t' *bribe* me?" Ten-Horse glowered.

Darst quit smiling suddenly and a shift in mood hung dark and heavy shadows across his cheeks. "It won't be necessary to bribe either you or anybody else. There are . . . other ways," he said.

"Why, you son of a Siwash!" Ten-Horse howled. "You open that place up again an' I'll send you so far, you'll look on Devil's Island as a place to live in luxury! I'll have you pickin' lint on the steppes of Siberia!"

Darst's pallid, highboned face went strictly grave. "Perhaps a new Sheriff will take a more lenient view of the situation," he murmured. "After all, no Sheriff is a permanent fixture."

"Well, you'll think so before you get me out," growled Ten-Horse, balling up his fists.

"It might not take so long as you imagine," Darst remarked, and closed the door behind him.

XXV

Ten-Horse Plays God— One Time!

"Any time a long-geared squirt like Deuces Darst kin slip the skids under me, I'll turn in my star an' take tuh plantin' grapefruits," Pony George commented as he and the Sheriff took seats at the Alamo's crowded counter.

"That guy," Ten-Horse told him, "ain't goin' t' put the skids under nobody—less'n it's himself. I wonder what he meant when he made that brag about me mebbe gettin' through quicker'n I expected? D'yuh reckon that coyote's been pullin' strings?"

"I wouldn't worry about it," George said airily.

"Well, I ain't. Imagine that sucker tryin' t' bribe me! You was wise not t' make no cracks in front of him about that guy you plugged. I wouldn't trust that gambler any farther'n I could sling a wasp by its tail!"

"Hell, I wouldn't trust him that far," George

197

declared. "When you figgerin' on pullin' in this Bandit?"

"Before tomorrow night, anyhow, if he's the bird you think. I'm goin' to take a li'l pasear after supper an' see what I can dig up. I figure to ramble out towards the Lazy D."

"Well, keep yore mind on yore business if yuh go out there," George admonished. "This ain't no time t' be thinkin' of gals."

"Huh!" said Ten-Horse, looking at him slanchways. "*You* sure ain't goin' t' have no time to squander that way. I want you t' circulate round town tonight an' see if you can get a line on our friend. Somethin' tells me he's goin' t' figger town as the best place fer him to spend the next few hours. If you come across him, don't do nothin' rash. Jest keep track of him till I get back. We don't want no slip-ups. Them County Comms is gettin' peeved."

Doris May came bustling forward and George's eyes signaled appreciation. She caught sight of him with Ten-Horse and was in the process of flashing her toothy smile, when George's glance fastened on something farther down the counter.

He stiffened, gulped, and looked again. All thought of grub and biscuit-shooters departed from his mind.

His eyes had not deceived him. It was that damned fellow in the derby hat!

"What's the matter with your friend?" demanded

Doris May of Ten-Horse. "I tossed him a smile an' the look he give me back would have froze an Eskimo. Ain't he speakin' to common folks no more?"

"I reckon he's workin' on that poem of his—he gets mighty puckery round the gills when he starts crankin' out them jingles," Ten-Horse chuckled, and wheeled around to see what effect his words had had on George.

He was just in time to see George's back as it vanished through the door.

"Well," he said, whipping his glance back up to Doris May; "that's funny." But the face of Doris May showed not a sign of humor, so he hastened to add: "Looks like he'd lost his appetite, or somethin'."

"Yes," said the handsome biscuit-shooter coldly; "it's too darn bad about him. A girl would think he was the only pebble on the beach, the way he acts. But I expect there are other males in circulation that're just as prominent as he is—an' a heap more easy on the eyes! He can take his poetry an' go to Jericho, for all of me! I'll get along!"

And off she sailed with a toss of the head, her chin held stormily high.

It was eight-fifteen when Ten-Horse left the restaurant and started up the street. He was accosted suddenly by George who bobbed up out of an alley.

"You'll get salivated someday, jumpin' out at a fella like that," growled Ten-Horse grumpily, shoving his gun back in leather. "Where in hell hev you been?"

"Oh, jest gallivantin' round," George answered vaguely. He came closer and with an anxious look peered up into the sheriff's face. "That fella quit the hash-house yet?"

"What fella?"

"That buzzard in the derby hat—that hard-eyed hombre that was on the jury the other day. Didn't yuh *see* him?"

Ten-Horse shook his head. Then, recalling that in the darkness George might not catch the gesture, he muttered, "No. What you worryin' about *him* for? He ain't involved in this, is he?"

"I don't know what he's involved in," George growled. irritably. "But he's a snoopin', sneakin' gumshoe or I'm a cockeyed Chinaman's gran'maw!"

Ten-Horse stared. "A *dick?* Now what in hell would a dick be doin'—*Oh!* Mebbe he's a pardner of that dick you was maulin' in my office."

George gulped and dragged a hand across his forehead. "Mebbe he is, at that. He's sure got himself int'rested in my movements, I know *that* much! That's the secon' time I caught that bozo sizin' me up. Third time's a charm, they say—I think I better drift."

"You ain't figurin' t' let a derby-hatted stranger

200

run you outa town, are you?" Ten-Horse asked in astonishment. "What was you up to before you left Pecos? Didn't rob no bank or nothin', did you?"

"Hell, no!" George denied emphatically. "But there ain't no tellin' what kinda charge them dang County Commissioners may 'a' ribbed up on me after I left Reeves County. They had it in for me!"

"Well, keep out of his way an' you'll be all right. But I wouldn't let it worry me. Jest go on about your business, an' if he gets tough I'll handle him. . . . Well, I'll be seein' you later. Reckon I better saddle up an' mosey towards the Lazy D. Keep your eyes peeled wide for our black-garbed friend an' don't make no crazy motions."

He left George then, abruptly, and struck off toward the public corral to get his horses.

It was a dark and windy night, with neither stars nor moon a-twinkle in that black, grim vault above. Ten-Horse, peering upward, wondered if it were going to rain. Seemed like it was getting too cold to rain, he reflected, and suddenly stopped his forward pacing, bringing up sharp and stiffening, that wind tortured cry still ringing in his ears.

He was almost abreast the alley running between the general store and Jeff Morris' Striped Tiger Bar. He felt sure the sound had come from there. But he was not certain.

He moved forward cautiously, one hand

dropping to the holstered Colt that rubbed his thigh.

The alley loomed darker than a stack of stovelids, and the gusty wind that ripped low whining sounds from the store roof's vigas reared unaccustomed shapes among its curdled shadows. Ten-Horse crouched there, moveless, his narrowed eyes probing for some sign.

The seconds dragged and Ten-Horse's shoulders stirred impatiently. He'd better investigate, he thought; for that cry he'd heard might have come from some inebriated puncher being rolled for what loose change might be found within his pockets.

He started forward.

There was a splash of flame from the alley's end. A slug bit past his shoulder crying *"Cousin!"* And a rifle's bark lashed out and beat against the building walls.

He heard the pound of running feet and dashed for the alley at the opposite side of Morris' Striped Tiger Bar to head the bush-whacker off. He reached it and went slopping down its murky length with red-eyed thoughts of vengeance. Wild fury pounded through his veins. They must think him a prize giraffe to be taken in by any such stunt as that! He gritted his teeth in dudgeon and went slamming round the saloon's far corner, skidding to a jarring stop.

There was not a sound to be heard save the

wind's eerie whisper among the cottonwoods. Ten-Horse strained his ears but caught no faintest echo of a bootstep.

"Where in hell has that whippoorwill gone?" he muttered, peering round among the flowing shadows. But nothing resembling a man's shape showed, and with an oath he mounted to the back room's door and banged his fist upon it.

The place was dark, but Jones' experience had taught him much concerning the rank deception of appearances. He pounded like hell's cook banging the gong for breakfast. And pretty soon a man's muted voice came through the barrier demanding to know who was there, and what the knocker thought he was up to.

"You'll find out what I'm up to!" Ten-Horse growled. "Is that you, Darst? Well, open up, dammit—what d'ye think I'm standin' here for, *my health?*"

"How do *I* know what you're out there for?" Darst answered, opening the door three cautious inches. "I don't even know it's *you*—an' if it ain't, whoever it is had better watch their onions. I got a hog-leg here an' I ain't a mite bashful about usin' it."

"Too darn bad about you! What's the matter—is your conscience botherin' you? C'mon, now, open up that door before I kick it in! This is the Law a-talkin'. My patience is plumb used up!"

Darst opened the door and Jones stepped in, his

gun held leveled and his finger curled round its trigger. "Reg'lar night owl, ain't you? What's the matter with your light?"

"Light?" Darst grunted. "What light?"

"I guess," sneered Ten-Horse insultingly, "you're one of them gents as does his sittin' in the dark. Either that or you got somethin' you're tryin' t'hide. Git a lamp goin'."

"All right," Darst said. "I'll have one in a minute," and Jones could hear him walking around and fumbling with something that might well indeed have been the mantle he claimed to be in search for. "Reason I didn't come sooner, or have a lamp lit out here, was 'cause I been settin' in the other room, he added.

"What—in that empty barroom? Well, there wasn't no light in there, either."

"No," Darst said. "I was in there gettin' a drink. I don't need no light for that."

He struck a match, snapped the mantle about the flaring flame, and adjusted the wick. Then he lifted the lamp up to its bracket and swung round facing Jones with a scowl.

"I'll sure be glad when this town catches up to the rest of the country. I'm gettin' plenty sick of drinkin' alkali water an' readin' by a lamp."

"There's a lot worse things than them in this bloody world," Ten-Horse told him darkly. "Where was you before you went in the barroom for that drink?"

"Say, what is this anyway—a inquisition?" Darst demanded.

"You'll think so if you don't start findin' answers for my questions. C'mon, now; where was you before you went in after that drink?"

"I was upstairs taking a nap."

"Oh, yeah? S'pose I was t' tell you you was out back of that alley that runs up 'longside the general store?"

The gambler laughed. "I'd say you been drinkin' better stuff than I been. Where'd you get that crazy notion?"

Ten-Horse said nothing, but with a tightening of his grim-lipped mouth strode over to the barroom door. It stood ajar, and just beyond it the lamp-light's reaching yellow radiance disclosed a longish gleam of metal. Thrusting his hand around the doorframe Ten-Horse brought to view a rifle.

He stood there holding it awhile, not saying anything, but eying the gambler with a reticent regard.

So long-maintained and steady was this look that Darst's shoulders twitched impatiently, and his pale, lean cheeks took on a sullen contour. "Well," he snapped, "what the hell's the matter with you?"

"Nothing," Ten-Horse drawled. "But was I you, I believe I'd put that hog-leg down. Just for the sake of health an' amity, you know. Sometimes a gent will find that holdin' a loaded pistol while another hombre's round, kinda gets to workin' on a fella's imagination. Most anythin's like t' happen. An'," he added softly, "I'd hate t' be responsible for what might happen t' you should your trigger-finger get a sudden itchin'."

Darst scowled, then sneered and put his gun away.

"That's better," Ten-Horse said, and sheathed his own.

He lifted up the rifle then and squinted down its barrel, but with a weather eye still cocked upon the gambler. "Huh," he murmured gruffly, and lowered the gun, sliding back its bolt and sniffing at the breech. "Hmm," he muttered, looking up. "Is this your rifle, Darst?"

"Sure—an old one I keep round for decoration. Haven't used the thing in years. Didn't even know it was back here—"

"Haven't used the thing in years, eh?" Ten-Horse interrupted. "How-come, then, the barrel's warm an' I can smell smoke an' there's powder particles stickin' to the bore?"

Darst looked startled. "Is there?"

Ten-Horse nodded. "This weapon's just been fired. Have you had a lapse of mem'ry?"

A trace of red showed thinly at the tips of the gambler's ears. "I haven't touched that gun," he said, "for more'n three weeks."

Ten-Horse stared. "Now listen, Darst. You talk an' talk damn quick or I'll slap you in the cooler till you do. I'm gettin' plumb fed up with this stuff. If you didn't fire that gun, who did?"

"I don't know. I didn't even know the gun was back here. I lent it to Kinch Lee three weeks ago. He said there was a—"

"I ain't interested in what he said. Has Lee been round tonight?"

He was here a little while ago. He come upstairs an' woke me up. Wanted to know could I lend him fifty dollars. When he left I come down to get that drink."

"That's your story, is it?"

"What's the matter with it?"

Ten-Horse grinned malignantly. "Somebody," he said, "just took a shot at me with a rifle. An' if I don't find Lee in town I'm comin' back an' shove you in for attempted murder—just dream awhile on that!"

Though he raked the town with a fine-toothed comb, neither Ten-Horse nor his deputy found trace of the Bar X owner. If he'd come in this night at all, he'd certainly gotten clean away. They saw no sign of Sumptor's burly foreman, either. Then they went to the Striped Tiger after Darst, and drew another blank. Darst had gone, and cleaned the safe in passing; plainly he'd seen the writing on the wall and was headed for greener pastures.

Ten-Horse swore in a passion.

But he swore louder and more furiously when

George, exploring the murk of that alley from which the sniper had fired his rifle, stumbled across an outsprawled body. The man was Slow Jim Hart, and he was very dead.

XXVI

"Don't Ever Speak to Me Again!"

"Oh, Ten-Horse!—*Wait!*"

Jones and Pony George had just reached the Sheriff's Office and had been about to mount the steps. But sound of that urgent voice now turned them swiftly in their tracks.

George took one look at the approaching horsemen. "Here comes trouble, hombre—take it from a man what knows! When a dame starts chasin' after yuh, that's when it's time tuh pull in yore horns an' make a dust fer other parts!"

Ten-Horse scowled, but made no answer. He leaned his gaunt shape against a corner of the building and waited for Tumbleweed Sumptor's daughter to come up.

She did so, and sat there in the light from the office window looking down at him expectantly, with one knee curled about the saddle horn and her reins loosely grasped in a gloved left hand.

But Ten-Horse Jones was mighty tuckered and

cross and baffled, and no smile lighted up his dusty face.

"Aren't you going to say hello?" she asked. "Or take off your hat, or something?"

Jones stared up at her grimly. " 'Fraid not," he answered bluntly. "I'm pretty busy, kid; so speak what's on your mind an' don't bother 'bout the trimmin's."

Was ever remark better calculated to defeat its very purpose? Certainly it was far from the way a man of the Sheriff's sentiments might be expected to address that lady for whom those sentiments had been professed. In matter of time, but a handful of hours had elapsed since Jones had declared undying admiration and love not bounded even by the oceans. Furthermore, and in particular since she had just ridden more than twenty miles to bring him information she had reason to believe he stood in need of, Antonia Sumptor was not the girl to take any such cavalier treatment lying down.

"Is that so?" she flared. "It's just too bad about you, now, isn't it! Who do you think you are? I've a darned good mind to let you stew in you own juice! Here I've ridden clear from the ranch to do you a favor an' you treat me like a banker's poor relation! I guess—"

"Shucks, I'm sorry, Tony," Ten-Horse said contritely. "I expect my temper's kinda frazzled. Ol' Lady Luck's been leerin' down 'er nose at me. Kick me, if it'll make things right between us."

And he made as though to present that portion of his anatomy.

But Tony Sumptor said, "If I thought I could kick any sense in you, I would! What you need, Ten-Horse Jones, is to get some of the colossal conceit knocked out of you. I reckon then you'd be almost human."

George snickered. And Ten-Horse said, "Go ahead, gal; rub it in. I guess I got it comin'." Then, soberly, he asked: 'What was you wantin' to tell me?"

She eyed him for several moments before she finally spoke. She sat so long in silence that her horse stirred restlessly under her and she pulled him up with a tightened rein.

"I overheard a couple things last night—*where,* I'll not be mentioning. But there's trouble brewing for a friend of yours and I thought you'd ought to know. Some folks are plotting—"

Ten-Horse nodded sourly. "You coulda saved yourself the trouble. I guess I know the *friend* you mean. I thought you'd gotten over that; but I see you're still in a lather about him."

He looked at her resentfully, thrusting his hands far down in his pockets. "You said true words when you mentioned my 'colossal' conceit; no one but a drivelin' fool like me could ever hev imagined that you'd fallen for him! I sure take the medal for a prize baloney!"

"Ten-Horse Jones!" she cried out furiously. Are you insinuating—?"

"I'm way past that stage," he growled. "I got my eyes open now, an'—hell! You better prepare yourself for a shock, gal. We found him out in that alley back of the Striped Tiger 'bout an hour ago. You can find him over at Doc Millbane's funeral parlors."

"Find who? What in the world are you talking about?"

"Your boy-friend—Slow Jim Hart!"

Tony Sumptor gasped. In the light from the office window they saw her face go white and red.

Ten-Hose was grinning maliciously when without warning she leaned abruptly forward in her saddle and quirted him furiously across the face. "You ignorant brush-popper!" she cried out hotly. "Don't ever speak to me again!"

XXVII

Gunsmoke

"Yuh know," said George some fifteen minutes later, "if you'd quit stewin' 'bout the fickelness an' ongratefulness of female critters in gen'ral an' Tony Sumptor in pa'tic'lar fer about five seconds, an' concentrate on what c'ld be deduced from this yere sits-ee-ashun, we might git some place—or hev yuh lost all int'rest in that Bandit?"

Ten-Horse pivoted wickedly and glared. "If you got anythin' t' say, then *say* it!"

"Did yuh notice that bronc Sumptor's kid was ridin'?"

"What about it?"

"Sleek. An' black. An' a geldin', wa'n't it?"

Ten-Horse stiffened in his tracks. A great light broke across his face. "Do you suppose—?" he started slowly. He did not wait for an answer, but shook his head emphatically. "Nope—you're havin' a pipe dream, George. There's nothin' to it. In the first place, if that was the horse, they'd never 'a' left it where Tony would be like t' saddle it an' go ridin' it round the country. The fellas back of this ain't simple, George—"

"They was simple enough t' try t' bush-whack you tonight, wasn't they?"

"That was diff'rent. But this horse—Nope, it just ain't possible."

"Ain't, eh?" George sat down upon the desk and grinned maliciously. "Look—you been oratin' how yuh'd humble Tony Sumptor if 'twas the las' thing yuh ever did. Wal, here's yore chance; it sure would humble her t' hev her ol'man sent t' the pen fer murder, wouldn't it? Dang well right it would!"

"Mebbe so. But you're all wet about that horse, George. It just ain't possible—an' even if it *was*

212

the Bandit's nag, it wouldn't prove nothin'. An' if it did, I wouldn't have the heart—"

"No, you blasted sizzle-pants! Yuh're jest a windbag four-flush like young Hart—!"

"Who's a sizzle-pants? *Who's* a windy four-flush?" Ten-Horse bellowed, striding forward furiously.

"You are!" George spat back. "You let that Sumptor kid use language on you I wouldn't take off my wife—if I was crazy enough t' hev one! Yuh let 'er quirt yuh like a blasted peon! Why, she treated you like *dirt!*"

They glared across three inches of furious silence. Both had their jaws thrust forward and cheeks pulled taut. Both had their knuckles bunched for battle. Ten-Horse towered above his deputy like he meant to throttle him.

But George wasn't backing down.

He said: "D'yuh think I'd let any coupla yards o' calico dress *me* down like that? Wal, not so's you c'ld notice it! Take that daggone biscuit-shooter at the Alamo—didn't she ack like somebody'd sprinkled ground glass in her frostin' when I breezed outa there t'night? *Sure* she did! But yuh don't see me go moochin' round t' git back in 'er graces! By cripes, I got a bone in my spinal column! These women're are alike! Blow hot, blow cold! A bunch o' dadburned weather-vanes! The less yuh hev t' do with 'em, the better off yuh are! If you got a ounce o' gumpshun

213

yuh'll go out t' the Lazy D an' 'rest the lot of 'em! It's ol'man Sumptor what's back of these killin's, an' you know it sure as I do!"

"You got anythin' t' base that on?" gruffed Ten-Horse, red to his ears.

"Yuh're bloomin' right I hev! That hawse the gal was forkin'! An' other things! Didn't she claim to've *overheard* a thing or two? Didn't she say she'd rid clear from the *ranch* t' warn yuh? What more d'you want? If you can't add that up an' spell Sumptor, then I'm a pot-eyed Chinaman!"

"You'll get my version of your pedigree *later,*" Ten-Horse growled. "But right now I'll take you up on this, an' if you've slipped someplace, Gawd help you! Now let's have the rest of this; what makes you think Sumptor's back of these killin's?"

"It ain't jest Sumptor," George declared. "It's Sumptor, Darst, an' that 'bino-eyed Kinch Lee! I figure them an' Dunkett hung ol'Hart. Then mebbe Sumptor figured Dunkett'd squeal, so knifed him to shut his mouth. Darst wa'nt around town last night, an' coupled with what the gal jest told yuh, I reckon there was a conference at Sumptor's. He prob'ly passed the word aroun' t' git Slow Jim. Don't ast me *why!* First place, I don't give a damn! I got a hunch, an' I'm backin' 'er to the limit!"

"All right," Ten-Horse growled. "I'll trail along. You get your bronc an' sashay out t' Bloody Run

Canyon an' keep your eye skinned for that Bandit. Don't make no plays, but if you locate him come for me! I'll be out at the Lazy D if you can't find me here in town!"

"What I want t' know," Sumptor snarled, "is where that goddam girl has got to! She was here this mornin'—"

"She's prob'ly gone to town to do some shoppin'," Kinch Lee soothed. "I can't see as her absence is anythin' to go gettin' lathered—"

"You couldn't see a monkey in a snowdrift!" Sumptor sneered. "I'm tellin' you things ain't goin' right! There's a feel of danger in the air—I been feelin' it all day. There's somethin' goin' to happen an' I know I ain't goin' t' like it! For one thing, that bustard, Jones, is gettin' too damn smart! *He's* the one—or his deputy, which is all the same—that put me wise to that stunt you pulled with them cattle! He didn't do that out love for me. He's got somethin' up his sleeve an'—"

"I heard in town this noon," Lee muttered, "that he's gettin' sweet on Tony. All but kissed her the other night in front of them loafers that's always warmin' the porch of Keefer's store."

Sumptor swore. "I'll tan her hide when she gits back!" he threatened. "No kin o' mine can go round lallygoshin' like a common strumpet! By Gawd, I got a man picked out for—"

He broke off and whirled, his hand going downward for his gun, as boots stamped echoes from the ranch house porch.

The door swung open and Darst ducked in, brushing past Kinch Lee as though he were not there; pulling up in front of Sumptor and breathing fast. He looked on edge, and all his movements held a nervous quickness. The eyes he fixed on Sumptor held a strange, unhealthy glimmer.

"Well," he rasped; "I've done your chore—an' by Christ it'll be the last one! I'm pullin' no more chestnuts out for *you!* Letters or no letters!"

"Is that so!" jeered Sumptor. "When I pop the whip you'll jump!"

"Not any more, I won't! I'm gettin' out of this country pronto. You can find some other fool t' be the monkey on your stick! I've killed Slow Jim—"

"Well, *that's* something." Sumptor's shaved hog features relaxed a little, and he started one hand toward his pocket. "You get a bonus outa—"

"Keep yore goddam bonus!" the gambler gritted, curling back his lips. "An' keep yore hand away from that *gun* or I'll blow yore bloody light!"

Sumptor's hand stopped where it was. His fat roan cheeks showed derisive humor, but the depths of his eyes were hard and bright, and his shoulders bowed a little forward as though he were tired and about to turn away.

But if such had been his intention Darst's voice

stopped him, even as a moment before it had stopped his hand's descent. *"Don't move!"* Darst said it wickedly, and with his words hardly more than a whisper. "I'm doin' the orderin' now, an' by Gawd I'll be obeyed. Sing out the combination of that safe."

A rash grin tightened the line of Sumptor's lips. "Do you think you can get away with this—?"

"I'm *gettin'* away with it. Let's have that combination now. Take it down, Lee, an' go an' check it. We're all through playin' this Big-Shot's game. We're splittin' this swag right now, an' then I'm dustin'."

The smile wiped off of Sumptor's features. There was a hard look about his eyes. "By Gawd, you go too far, Deuces! You'll never—"

"I'll be the judge o' that," Darst choked him off. "Just unreel that combination, *An' I won't be askin' you again!*"

Sumptor reeled off a bunch of numbers, his expression like that of a coiling snake.

Anger abruptly got away with him. Destructive purpose brightened the blue of his flaring gaze.

One hand was almost at his hip when flame spurted from the gambler's gun. The slug's force smashed him back against the wall.

The expression of Sumptor's face was awful in that moment. His eyes seemed almost bursting from his head. And the arm that had thrust the hand at his pistol now hung limp and without direction.

But the sure hard way that was his manner had not been jarred from the rancher. His big, rolling shoulders looked massive yet, and power still hung about him like a cloak.

His eyes squeezed down to glittering slits, and he leered across the crimson that was spreading on his shirtfront. He said with an explosive burst of breath, *"By Gawd—"*

Darst caught his gaze and flung a swift look toward the door. Kinch Lee, from his crouched position before the safe, looked up and followed the focus of their gaze. And his form, too, went stiff as Darst's. And the color drained completely from his features.

It was a startling thing!

The door stood wide, and in it, framed against the night, the black clothes lending his tautened features the pallor of one new-risen from the grave, stood Tucker Hart.

Sumptor stared, and a shudder pulsed throughout his body. Darst went gray and breath burst from him like a sob. Kinch Lee recoiled and breaking from his crouch came upright, shrinking back against the safe. The chattering of his teeth made a sound like castanets.

They seemed to know this was no living man who stood before them. The gun drooped low in Darst's cold hand.

Sumptor dragged a sleeve across his forehead. Blood from his battered chest was forming a pool between his feet. He whispered hoarsely:

"Hart! By Gawd, it can't be . . ."

"But it *is*—you're starin' Death right in the face, gents. I told you I'd come back, an' here I am." A gun was leveled from the still hand resting against Hart's thigh.

"By Gawd, we *hung* you!" Sumptor gritted. "You *can't* be here—*get away!*"

"You hung me, yeah—in one almighty hurry! 'F you'd taken the time t' search me an' hadn't been in such a lather to git elswhere, you'd a found Jim's knife where 'twas stickin' in the back o' my belt! I damn' near cut yore rope through 'fore yuh rattled outa sight! It's sure a lesson for yuh— never do a chore unless yuh plan t' do it well."

"It'll *be* done better this time!" Kinch Lee choked, and brought his gun up spitting fire.

But Old Hart laughed. The pistol bucked against his palm and Lee went down with a dark hole between his bursting eyes.

Darst brought his gun up with a curse. He pivoted with white flame tearing from his other hand. But the swift trip-hammer beat of Old Hart's roaring weapon rolled across this room like the boom of surf against a reef.

Darst reeled sideways, caught himself against the wall, and fired again. But his bullet stubbed the floor. And a moment later he was on his hands and knees above it, slumping suddenly forward as though to hide the place.

With sheer brute will, and with the cold sweat pouring from his forehead, Sumptor got a gun in hand and worked it. He saw Darst fall, but paid him no attention. All his energies, every nerve in that great mountainous body, seemed bent on beating down this white-haired Hart who had ever been his Nemesis.

Powdersmoke lay across this room like fog—like a blue and acrid fog through which the lightning flash of six-guns sheared with wicked intent.

Hart staggered, swayed against the door. Once more the gun came up and steadied at his thigh. He squeezed the trigger on an empty chamber; dropped the pistol without change of expression, and procured another as though by magic from the region of his waist.

Again and yet again he drove its bullets smashing against the barrier of Sumptor's rock-like form.

As the reverberating echoes droned away the hinges of Sumptor's knees collapsed. He went down heavily and lay there shuddering while his pistol clattered on the floor beside his hand.

Tucker Hart went reeling forward and stood there swaying groggily while he stared with bitter eyes upon his brother. "Stud of a bastard breed," he whispered; "may the old Adam burn yore soul in hell!"

Long after Sumptor's boots had ceased their

drumming, Old Hart stood there. Old memories had thrown their pictures on the curtain of his mind. He saw the old Wyoming cow-spread—saw it now as others had seen it in those long-past days: a handy relay for longriders. He recalled the murdered sheriff left one night in its front yard by this treacherous black-sheep brother who had never brought the family aught but grief. He remembered the arrest and conviction that had followed on its heels—the jail break he had managed after three hard years of hell. And those months of flight when he had kept a saddled bronc ever at his hand, and the leanness and futility of those days and that existence. Then the new blow struck with the staggering discovery of his loved wife's death. The long night ride with the motherless boy who was now Slow Jim. . . .

He remembered reaching Texas. Start of a new life. The arrival of this brother at the border, tagged by the dust of Mexican Rurales. Tumbleweed's capture, and his own subsequent refusal to lift a hand in that black sheep's defense.

And here on this grimy floor lay that brother's body in a pool of thickening blood.

As though from some great distance it seemed to Hart a feminine voice was calling . . . calling him. A voice that was filled with an eager hope and cheer.

Slowly he straightened up. A smile got on his

lips and content came into his heart . . . the first he'd known in years.

His lips moved; their words were hardly audible. "I'm coming, Mother! Coming. . ."

Still smiling, Tucker Hart lurched forward, and fell across his brother's body and lay still.

XXVIII

"Fly at It!"

Ten-Horse Jones came out of the house with hot, moist eyes, and both fists tightly clenched within his pockets. He'd arrived in time to take in most of what had happened in this long main room of Sumptor's ranch house; he had come, in fact, on the heels of Tucker Hart. But what had taken place had happened too suddenly for him to intervene. He was in a moochin' frame of mind and filled with turbulence. The surprise of finding Hart alive had incapacitated him for action until all need for it had passed in the crashing thunder of those belching guns.

He blamed himself for Old Hart's death and cursed with wicked fury.

The staccato drumming of a fast-moving horse beat against his ears with increasing nearness; but went unheeded. His mind was too filled with this thing that he'd just witnessed. He could not orient himself, though an edge of his thinking warned him of the possible danger in this unknown rider's approach.

He had known Hart for several years, and liked him. Grim and hard, the old man was; a man who'd fight for his rights to the last damned ditch—yet withal the kind who'd take the shirt right off his back should he find a man whose need was greater. Ten-Horse had heard from time to time the sundry rumors wafted round concerning Hart's never-mentioned past; but had put no credence in them. He has taken the man for what he'd found him and had felt no curiosity concerning those things the grim old man had kept beneath his hat.

"That you, Ten-Hawse?"

It took the sheriff another moment to realize that all sound of hoofs had ceased. In its place had come the wheeze of heavy breathing, a creak of saddle leather, and a voice that kept on doggedly asking: "That you, Ten-Hawse?"

He wheeled round now and put a narrowed glance upon the yonder horseman where he sat his bronc in the moon's illumination a pace or two before the alder's grotesque shadow.

He recognized George then, and swore.

"Wa'n't that shootin'—?" George began.

"Listen!" Ten-Horse cut him off. "Thought I told you t' go rammin' round that canyon hideout of the Bandit!"

" 'S what I *been* doin'," George said grumpily. "An' believe me, I sure got results! Hid out in that dang rockpile no'th of the canyon entrance—an' daggone lucky that I did! I lit out soon's he cleared, an' I been ridin' hellity-larrup ever sinct!"

"Quit squawkin' riddles an' try the English language for a change," growled Ten-Horse.

"Wal," George sniffed, "in the words of the 'mortal Shaks-Pur, I seen a fella ride outen that canyon 'long about dusk; towin' a hawse with a tied girl in the saddle. Had 'er gagged an' both arms looped over a stick behind her back an' tied in front of her. 'Twas Tony Sumptor. An' the—"

In two bounds Ten-Horse got to George and yanked him from the saddle. He shook him like a rag-stuffed doll. "Bite it out," he snapped, "an never mind that goddam literary millinery! Who was the man? An' where the hell is he *now?*"

"It was Bill McCash," George gulped, "an' he's headin' fer the Mexican Line!"

False dawn was just flushing the ragged eastern skyline, vesting each crag and upthrust butte with the grotesque contours of vague and massive prehistoric mammals, when Ten-Horse turned his band of snorting broomtails down a narrow valley winding between the towering bastions of Eagle Mountain and the scattered volcanic crags of the grim Van Horns, and paused to scan the fog-filled forward reach.

Ghostly and tenuous, the stringers of drifting mist were swirling in the quickening breeze like a pot of smoke being laved by the Devil's ladle. Some places Ten-Horse could get but little view of the terrain beyond, but in others, where the gathered vapor lay less thick and its wet white blanket was being ripped by the morning wind, he could glimpse long vistas of the rolling valley floor.

Long and searchingly his squinted eyes probed those yonder lanes. And just before night's last darkness brushed across the land he spied his quarry. Two slowly-moving darker specks against horizon's murk.

They seemed slow-moving, but he knew this for an illusion squired by distance. He guessed that they were traveling fast, not putting too much trust in their certain lead, nor banking too strongly on the possibility of Tony's not yet having been missed. McCash was too astute a hand to be taking any chances he could avoid.

Ten-Horse judged their lead to be about three miles. He gritted his teeth in a rage. The Border was a bare eight miles away, and they were three miles nearer it than he. He cursed with passion as he slid from his bronc and climbed the saddle atop another's back. Then his quirt swung down in a whistling arc and his spurs drew blood for the first time in this startled broomtail's memory.

Into the lifting fog they charged, and on through

its darkened white mantle with the cold wind rushing in their ears. On they swept, like eagles in full flight over that long dark level that stretched so desolately between them and the Bandit of Bloody Run and the girl his evil lust had bidden him take across the Border.

Twenty minutes passed without other sound than the steady throbbing of pounding hoofs and the wild shrill whistle of the wind as they rushed against it headlong. Then Ten-Horse swung his bronc alongside another and swapped saddles without so much as breaking stride.

On and on and on they plunged, rocketing recklessly into the dark unknown beyond the swirling fog's thick gloom. And Ten-Horse's right arm rose and fell with wearying regularity. If he had to kill every horse in his string, he meant to come up with Bill McCash for a final accounting before he reached that Border!

They went ramming into the mouth of a gorge; it loomed like the portal of Hell's abyss. But Ten-Horse drove his broncos down it like a man possessed, and cursed with raucous fury each time a broomtail strove to turn aside.

On and on and on they sped while the true dawn rose and the sun flung its first bright shafts across that yonder sawtoothed rim.

Out of the gorge they flashed and into a widening canyon. The clatter of their headlong pace roused up the echoes and lashed them back and forth between the granite walls. Not a moment's respite did Ten-Horse give his horses; not one faltering stride did he allow them. Each time a mount's tired muscles showed in lagging legs, he went hurtling to another's back and the wild grim chase went on.

The east glowed bright. The magic of the mighty sun spread a bank of orange color across the tawny earth, and to each side the mountains' rugged slopes stood sharp and clear.

But Ten-Horse had no interest in the marvel of this spectacle. All his energies were bent in one direction—forward! And his eyes were fiercely riveted to the silhouetted horseman that stood out stark against the plain a mile away.

Once more Ten-Horse changed his saddle. Luckily the wind was blowing toward him from the gulches of Old Mexico across the Rio Grande. Bill McCash had not yet observed him and was proceeding southward at a slower gait.

Ten-Horse lashed his four remaining broomtails onward, tightened the chin-strap of his Stetson, and went plowing on. His other horses had dropped out of the chase, but it was in his mind that the four remaining would prove ample to carry him within pistol shot of the fleeing renegade.

Then, suddenly, he saw McCash's mount go down in a staggering fall. He saw McCash leap clear and go bounding up behind the girl in a way that showed him McCash had discovered he was being followed. The flashing of McCash's big spurs and the steady downward slashing of his stout right arm were proof in plenty.

On they raced for another quarter hour; McCash doing his utmost on his overburdened pony to beat Jones to those gulches and ravines across the river, and Ten-Horse equally determined that he should not succeed.

Ten-Horse swapped his saddle for that atop a horse in his dwindled string that had not yet been ridden. The comparative freshness of this new bronc began to swiftly tell. Length by length they closed the distance separating themselves from the fleeing Bandit.

McCash abruptly gave over the beating of his bronc and dragged the carbine from its place beneath the stirrup leather. Twisting his black-clad form he turned a whitened face and clapped the saddle-gun to shoulder—*his left shoulder;* his right was bulky with a bandage. A flash belched out, a puff of smoke, and lead tore past the sheriff's head. The gun's report struck flatly across the early morning stillness.

Jones' thin lips streaked a smile. His pale eyes shone with a cold amusement. "Losin' his head, the fish-bellied shorthorn!"

McCash's horse had slowed to a lurching shuffle; it was foundering under its double load and the long night ride that lay behind it. It had given its best, but that best measured mighty short when stacked against the forty fast legs that Ten-Horse packed in his string.

McCash emptied his rifle and pulled his floundering broomtail to a stop. He slid from its back, shoving fresh cartridges in his rifle, and left it on braced and wabbly legs with its downflung head between its knees.

Ten-Horse saw McCash's dark figure limp stiff-legged a few short paces, then drop down upon one knee. He watched the carbine rise again and stock against a shoulder. He saw black-garbed McCash take careful aim.

His heart nearly stopped its beating as he watched that rifle's muzzle. All the odds had swung to McCash. But Ten-Horse Jones never slowed his pony's forward-hurtling pace a fraction. He watched with slitted eyes and his long grim jaw clamped tight.

And when fire spurted from the Bandit's weapon he ducked. Low down he swung upon the roan's offside. And flipping his pistol free he thrust its barrel beneath his bronc's extended neck and let drive with wicked fury.

The shot's effect was strong and instant.

McCash kept firing, but his shots went wild. He did not pause for aim again, but worked his gun as fast as he could squeeze the trigger. The droning of his lead whanged past long yards away. It looked mighty like McCash had lost his nerve!

"What you poppin' for—*the moon?*" yelled Ten-Horse fleetingly.

McCash came upright with an oath. He slammed his rifle down and scuttled for his horse. His arms flashed up and he dragged Tony roughly from the saddle, whirling savagely and swinging her round in front of him while his right hand clawed viciously at his hip.

Ten-Horse cursed with passion at the baseness of the man. "You hook-gutted worm!" he bellowed. "Git out from behind that petticoat an' take your medicine like a man!"

McCash said nothing. But flame belched from his hip as Ten-Horse left the saddle, lit on skidding bootheels, and went tearing forward in a cursing zigzagged crouch.

The first slug ripped at his hat. The second tugged his vest. The third ran a scorching line across his left ribs, momentarily throwing him out of stride. Then he dashed crazily on, red fury rioting in his brain, conscious of but one red-hot desire—the wish to get both hands about McCash's thick throat!

And then, abruptly, that spitting pistol of Bill McCash's went dry. The fact was evident by the look that flashed across his cheeks, by the teeth he suddenly bared, and by the frantic way his index finger kept clamping down on that trigger and only beating out a series of metallic clicks.

Ten-Horse had almost reached him when with

an oath he dropped the weapon and, flinging the girl away from him savagely, went sprinting for the crumbled lip of a dry wash several yards distant.

"Whoa up, you whippoorwill!" Ten-Horse blared. But McCash paid no attention.

Ten-Horse loosed a slug that kicked dust inches from the Bandit's pistoning boots. A second shot, driven almost instantly, ripped a whining sound through McCash's high-peaked black Stetson.

McCash swung round and, stopping, thrust both hands above his head.

"Stickin' them dew-claws up ain't buyin' you nothin' with *me!*" growled Ten-Horse. "Pull 'em down before I clip some fingers off!"

"What's the big idear, you stoppin' me this way?" McCash blustered, lowering his hands.

"That won't buy you nothin' neither," Ten-Horse rasped, with a sidelong glance to where the girl was struggling to her feet. You woman-stealin' hound! You oughta be boiled in sheep dip!"

"You goin' t' do the boilin'?" sneered McCash. He stood there in a graceful slouch and eyed Jones up and down.

Ten-Horse strode to within a couple of feet of him, his gun held rigid at his hip. Cold, alert and grim, he stood like some ominous statue of doom.

But McCash just sneered. "You ain't scarin' nobody, you blow-shoot fourflush. Any fool can stand there brave as blazes with a loaded smoke-pole stickin' in his fist!" He patted his own empty holster significantly. "You might not be lookin' so tough t' that calico 'f I had a gun in *my* paw."

Ten-Horse wasted no words. A second pistol appeared in his hand like magic. He shoved it at Bill McCash butt forward with a cold, sour smile that whitened the Lazy D foreman's cheeks.

"All right, you stage-robbin' woodchuck—fly at it!"

You could almost see McCash's paraded bravado wilt. The lines of his saturnine countenance were suddenly graven deeper. The boldness leaked from his glance and his eyes spread wide. You could catch the involuntary cringing of his muscles, and his tongue dashed nervously across his lips.

Bill McCash was afraid of Ten-Horse, and a man could see it though he strove to bolster up his pose with a pallid sneer. But he was scared to touch that gun the sheriff was holding out; twice he tentatively reached out a hand, but each time pulled it back without having touched the proffered butt.

"Take that gun, you chicken-livered polecat, 'fore I bend it across your scalp!"

Ten-Horse's hate was clearly mingled with the scathing contempt that stared from his level eyes. His rage was deep and bitter, but he could find no way to make the black-garbed Bandit join him in a shootout. McCash knew when he was beaten. He had no hankering to fight in open combat with a man like Ten-Horse Jones.

Jones returned one gun to his holster; the second weapon vanished as mysteriously as it had appeared. Motioning toward the staring, wide-eyed girl, he commanded curtly, "Untie her an' go catch up one of my horses for her." And, when McCash limped away, Jones added softly; "Any time you figger you got a break, hop to it."

But McCash wasn't doing any hopping.

He untied Tony and led up a saddled horse. He looked inquiringly at Jones.

"Catch up them others an' bring 'em here."

McCash did so.

Without looking at the girl Jones said, "Climb up. We're headin' back."

Tony got into the saddle stiffly. McCash turned to one of the two fresh horses and reached a hand up to the horn.

Ten-Horse said, "Not that one, hombre. Take that gentled one."

McCash eyed the tired bronc on which the sheriff had overtaken him, without favor. He muttered and swung to the saddle sullenly. Then—

"Let's go," Ten-Horse said.

XXIX

Ten-Horse Throws His Loop

They had covered some ten miles when Ten-Horse abruptly held his hand up, pulling his caballo to a halt. His narrowed eyes were grimly fixed to a distant rise atop which a dust had just now risen. Pulling his hatbrim lower he raked the ridge's near slope with probing gaze until he picked up the speeding dot that was a horseman. Hardly had he spotted the fellow before a second dust raced across the ridge-top.

" 'Pears like traffic's lookin' up," he muttered sourly.

Neither of his companions spoke. The girl flashed a covert glance to Ten-Horse's face. But Bill McCash stared straight ahead, and his glance was veiled with a studied inscrutability.

"We'll wait right here an' see this out," Ten-Horse decided.

He hooked a knee about the saddle horn and rolled himself a smoke left-handed while he watched the oncoming riders. Kind of seemed like the first man was running from the second, but no sign of gunsmoke blossomed for either rider.

Ten-Horse puffed his Durham in silence.

The girl dismounted, trailing her reins, and found a flat rock on which she sat near by in the scant shade offered by a giant cactus. Bill McCash displayed an Indian impassivity, sitting his saddle with folded arms, his gaze fixed straight ahead.

"That's George!" the girl cried suddenly, and Ten-Horse nodded.

"Sure," he said. "An' that other fella's a deputy from El Paso."

Fifteen minutes later George came larruping up and brought his bronc to a skidding halt in a cloud of dust. "Ten-Hawse," he panted heavily, "lemme hev a fresh nag quick! I gotta git across the Border!"

"What's the tearin' rush?" asked Ten-Horse mildly.

"Holy cow! Can't yuh see that sucker comin' after me?" cried George excitedly. "That's that derby-hatted vingaroon—"

"That," interrupted Ten-Horse, "is a dick from El Paso."

George swallowed noisily and gathered up his reins.

"Here—hold on," growled Ten-Horse. "He's out here for the Commissioners over at Reeves County. I had a talk with him yesterday morning. He ain't fixin' to arrest you. He's been huntin' you from hell to breakfast; the commissioners give him your description—"

"Hell's fire!"

Ten-Horse grabbed George by the arm as the latter's spur-prodded bronc went dashing past. They went down in a heap, and after Ten-Horse finally extricated himself and yanked George to his feet, he snarled, "For cripes sake, take it easy. Them Commissioners have got him lookin' for you because they've made up their confounded minds that you're the gent they want t' pack their sheriff's star!"

George's eyes were bulging in a way that far exceeded any surprise Ten-Horse's words might have been expected to create. Warning slapped the sheriff bang across the face. He dropped George's arm and whirled round just as the girl screamed: *"Ten-Horse!"*

Bill McCash had a gun in his fist, and its muzzle gaped like coast artillery straight at Ten-Horse's chest!

Flame spurted from two places. The double report cracked out like lightning. McCash had fired, but Ten-Horse's aim had been considerably the better. A dark spot bloomed on the Bandit's forehead. With a gasping sob he slid limply from his horse's back.

The derby-hatted dick came racing up. He took one look and grinned. "Congratulations, Jones," he said. "I couldn't of done a neater job myself. Looks like you're due fer a pot of money—the state's got plenty on that fella's scalp. He's wanted for about ten bank jobs besides this local stuff." He looked at George. "So this is Kasta," he said, grinning wryly. And then to Ten-Horse: "Want us to pack this fella in for you?"

Ten-Horse nodded.

About eight minutes later, when George and the dick and their grizzly burden turned off up an arroyo, the girl said shyly, "Ten-Horse, why didn't somebody tell me you were made of hero stuff?"

Ten-Horse snorted. "Hero stuff! That's good! There ain't no hero stuff in me! I do my duty as I see it, an' them that don't like it can take it on the lam!"

She leaned close, placing a hand upon his arm. "I'm truly sorry about our misunderstanding last night, and—and about those names I called you. I let my temper get away again; I've got an awful temper, Ten-Horse. . . ."

The fragrance of her mounted to his brain. He said: "I got a peach, myself. Shucks, I said a lot of things I didn't mean either. I—" Then suddenly he scowled.

"But even if you wasn't nuts about Slow Jim—"

"Slow Jim! Why, it's you I've been in love with all the time!"

Ten-Horse blinked. He passed a hand across his eyes. "Anyhow," he grunted dismally, "it's too late now. I didn't have nothin' to do with the shootin', but your Dad got rubbed out las' night in a shoot-out at the Lazy D—I went out there to arrest him—"

"But Tumbleweed Sumptor wasn't my Dad!" cried Tony softly. "Mother married twice—Tumbleweed was only my step-father. He—"

"Say!" Ten-Horse shouted. "Did you mean what you said a minute ago?"

"About lovin' you all the time?" There was a mischievous sparkle in Tony's eyes. "Well," she began judiciously, "possibly I was exaggerating somewhat—"

The rest was lost as Ten-Horse pulled her to him violently and kissed her full upon the mouth.

Center Point Large Print
600 Brooks Road / PO Box 1
Thorndike ME 04986-0001 USA

(207) 568-3717

US & Canada:
1 800 929-9108
www.centerpointlargeprint.com